Walter Chalmers Smith

Selections from the Poems of Walter C. Smith

Walter Chalmers Smith

Selections from the Poems of Walter C. Smith

ISBN/EAN: 9783744765152

Printed in Europe, USA, Canada, Australia, Japan

Cover: Foto ©Andreas Hilbeck / pixelio.de

More available books at **www.hansebooks.com**

CONTENTS.

Songs and Lyrics.

CONTENTS.

Character Sketches.

Descriptive Pieces.

SONGS AND LYRICS.

SHE IS A WOMAN TO LOVE.

SHE is a woman to love, to love
  As flowers love light ;
All that is best in you is at its best,
All the heart opens to her as a guest
  Who makes it bright.

She is a woman to love, to love
  With soul and heart;
And all in her that is sweet and true
She makes as if it were drawn from you
  By gracious art.

You cannot help but love, but love ;
  Nobody can ;
She carries a charm with her everywhere
Just a circle she makes in the air,
  Bewitching man.

A

Is it her beauty I love, I love?
  Is it her mind?
Is it her fancy, nimble and gay?
Or her voice that spirits the soul away?—
  I cannot find.

But she's just a woman to love, to love,
  As men love wine
Madly and blindly: yet why should they
Bring their hearts to be stolen away,
  When she has mine?

Borland Hall, p. 10.

SO SHE WENT DRIFTING.

So she went drifting, drifting
  Over the sea,
Thinking that others were shifting;
  Surely not she.
She no anchor had lifted,
  Meant not to move;
Only she slowly drifted
  Deep into love.

O she had held that a maiden
  Should not be first
To sigh with a heart love-laden,
  And long and thirst;
And mad at herself for her longing,
  Hard things she said,
Then was mad at herself for wronging
  The love she had.

He knew not how she was yearning
    Just for a word,
And went on his way discerning
    Nothing he heard :
Only he sometimes wondered
    What she could mean—
O had he only pondered
    He might have seen.

So she went drifting, drifting
    Day after day;
So he went shifting, shifting,
    Farther away ;
O but a word would have done it—
    Word never spoken ;
So she went drifting, drifting
    With her heart broken.

Borland Hall, p. 178.

WHAT HAS COME OVER THE SUNSHINE ?

WHAT has come over the sunshine?
    It is like a dream of bliss.
What has come over the pine-woods?
    Was ever a day like this?
O white-throat swallow flicking
    The loch with long wing-tips,
Hear you the low sweet laughter
    Comes rippling from its lips?

What has come over the waters?
  What has come over the trees?
Never were rills and fountains
  So merrily voiced as these.
O throstle softly piping
  High on the topmost bough,
I hear a new song singing,
  Is it my heart, or thou?

Kildrostan, p. 61.

ROW, BURNIE, ROW.

Row, burnie, row
  Through the bracken-glen ;
Row, burnie, row
  By the haunts of men ;
Where the golden cowslips glint,
Through the wild thyme and the mint,
By the barley and the lint ;
  Row, burnie, row.

Row, burnie, row
  Tinkling under heather bells ;
Row, burnie, row
  Down to where my true love dwells ;
Singing songs down to the sea,
Singing of the hill countrie,
Singing to my love from me :
  Row, burnie, row.

Row, burnie, row
  To him that's far awa,
Row, burnie, row,
  And mind him o' us a'.

Say there's naething I regret,
Say I never can forget,
Say I love him dearly yet:
  Row, burnie, row.

Row, burnie, row
  Through the gowans white,
Row, burnie, row,
  Gleaming in the light:
Let ilka ripple bear
Fond kisses to him there;
O my heart it's longing sair.
  Row, burnie, row.

Borland Hall, p. 148.

LOVE.

O WHAT is this that in my heart is singing,
  Like sweet bird, caged there, carolling all day?
O what is this such gladness to me bringing
  That life is bliss, and work is merry play,
And round my steps lo! sunny flowers are
    springing
  As I go singing, singing on my way?
    O Love, glad Love!

Ah! what is this that in my heart is sighing,
  Like captive vainly moaning to be free?
Ah! what is this so heavy in me lying,
  No rest there is, nor any work for me,
And leaf and flower are drooping now and dying
  As I go sighing, sighing wearily?
    O Love, sad Love!

What thing is this my foolish heart is dreaming,
  That I should love, and long for yon bright
    star?
I sigh or sing, but she, unmoved, is gleaming
  As in high glory where the angels are—
I but a glow-worm on the earth dull-beaming,
  While she is gleaming, gleaming there afar.
    O Love, vain Love !

                    Raban, p. 38.

MYSIE GORDON.

Now where is Mysie Gordon gone?
  What should take her up the glen,
Turning, dowie and alone,
  From smithy lads and farming men?—
    Never seen where lasses, daffing
    At the well, are blithely laughing,
    Dinging a' the chields at chaffing:
    Bonnie Mysie Gordon.

Mysie lo'ed a student gay,
  And he vowed he lo'ed her well :
She gave all her heart away,
  He lo'ed naething but himsel' :
    Then he went to woo his fortune,
    Fleechin', preachin', and exhortin',
    Got a Kirk, and now is courtin'—
    But no his Mysie Gordon.

Every night across the moor,
  Where the whaup and peewit cry,
Mysie seeks his mither's door
  Wi' the saut tear in her eye.

Little wots his boastfu' Minnie,
Proud to tell about her Johnnie,
Every word's a stab to bonnie
   Love-sick Mysie Gordon.

A' his letters she maun read,
  A' about the lady braw ;
Though the lassie's heart may bleed,
  Though it even break in twa ;
    Wae her life may be and weary,
    Mirk the nicht may be and eerie,
    Yet she'll gang, and fain luik cheerie,
      Bonnie Mysie Gordon.

Whiles she thinks it maun be richt ;
  She is but a landward girl ;
He a scholar, and a licht
  Meikle thocht o' by the Earl.
    Whiles she daurna think about it,
    Thole her love, nor live without it,
    Sair alike to trust, or doubt it,
      Waesome Mysie Gordon.

Mysie doesna curse the cuif,
  Doesna hate the lady braw,
Doesna even haud aloof,
  Nor wish them ony ill ava :
    But she leaves his proudfu' mither,
    Dragging through the dowie heather
    Weary feet by ane anither ;
      Bonnie Mysie Gordon.

Borland Hall, p. 17.

THE GIPSY GIRL.

MOTHER, O mother, I've put away
Velvet and silk for the raploch grey:
    Love is best!
Mother, O mother, my wedding ring
Hangs on the glass by a silken string:
    Golden chains are heavy.

Mother, O mother, if I could find
The rags that once fluttered in rain and wind—
    Love is best!
Mother, O mother, the rags were true—
And O that I had not listened to you:
    Golden chains are heavy.

Mother, O mother, who led the way
To the men who came from the ship in the bay?
    Love is best!
Mother, O mother, shell and shot
Pitied him whom you pitied not.
    Golden chains are heavy.

Mother, O mother, he did not die;
He is coming again to me by and bye.
    Love is best!
Mother, O mother, I love him still,
And if he says, Come to me, come I will.
    Golden chains are heavy.

Mother, O mother, I heard the cry
Of a baby, all night, that was hard to die. .
    Love is best!

Mother, O mother, my heart is wild,
And what shall I say when he asks for his child?
    Golden chains are heavy.

Mother, O mother, your lordling gay
Was wronged by my coming, not going away ;
    Love is best !
Mother, O mother, the woods are green,
Yet it never can be as it once has been.
    Golden chains are heavy.

Borland Hall, p. 122.

UP IN THE NORTH.

UP in the North, up in the North,
There lies the true home of valour and worth ;
Wild the wind sweeps over moorland and glen,
But truth is trusty, and men are men,
And hearts grow warmer the farther you go,
Up to the North with its hills and snow.
        Ho ! for the North, yo ho !

Out of the North, out of the North,
All the free men of the nations came forth ;
Kings of the sea, they rode, like its waves,
Crash on the old Roman empire of slaves,
And the poor cowed slaves and their Cæsars saw
Rise from its ruins our Freedom and Law.
        Ho ! for the North, yo ho !

Up in the North, up in the North,
O but our maids are the fairest on earth,

Simple and pure as the white briar-rose,
And their thoughts like the dew which it clasps
    as it blows;
There are no homes but where they be,
Woman made home in the north countrie.
    Ho! for the North, yo ho!

O for the North, O for the North!
O to be there when the stars come forth!
The less that the myrtle or rose is given,
The more do we see there the glory of heaven;
And care and burden I leave behind
When I turn my face to the old North wind.
    Ho! for the North, yo ho!

Borland Hall, p. 12.

THE FALSE SEA.

I.

SINGING to you,
And moaning to me;
Nothing is true
In the false, cruel sea.
Where its lip kisses
The sands, they are bare,
Where its foam hisses,
Nothing lives there;
When it is smiling,
Hushed as in sleep,
It is beguiling
Some one to weep.

II.

They were seafaring,
With light hearts and free,
And full of the daring
That's bred of the sea :
It crept up the inlet,
And bore them away
Where it laughed in the sunlight,
And dimpled the bay,
Singing to them,
But moaning to me,
Tripping it came,
The cold, cruel sea.

III.

I heard the oars dipping,
I heard her bows part
The waves with a rippling
That went through my heart.
And I saw women weeping
And wringing their hands
For the dead that were sleeping
That night on the sands :
For nothing is true
In the false, cruel sea,
Which is singing to you,
And moaning to me.

Borland Hall, p. 21.

THE HOURS.

BROWN, gipsy hours, with white teeth laughing
    gay,
Came trooping by me, when a child at play,
And with their coaxing stole my life away
Where bird in bush was idling all the day.

Soft, roguish hours, that in the gloaming peep
At woodland nooks a dewy tryste to keep,
Stole my young life away, and in a heap
Of rose leaves, sweetly smelling, hid it deep.

Dark, robber hours, like burglars in the night,
They broke into my house, by cunning sleight,
And bound me fast, as with a spell of might,
And reft my life away ere morning light.

The idle bird is silent on the tree,
The rose leaves withered now and scentless be,
The spell is broken; lo! mine eyes can see—
O thievish hours that stole my life from me!

Lost, lost! and now the mists, low trailing, screen
The visioned glories that I once have seen,
And all the hours are grey and cold and mean—
Lost, lost my life—and O the might have been!

Borland Hall, p. 39.

LATE, LATE IN MAY.

LATE, late in May the hawthorn burst in bloom,
Long searched by chill blasts from the nipping
    East ;
Late, late the fire-balls flamed upon the broom,
And golden-barrëd bees began to feast.

Late, late the blue-bells in the forest glade
Made skyey patches, starred with primrose sheen,
And lady-ferns, uncoiling in the shade,
Turned serpent-folds to plumes of waving green.

Late, late the bright fringe tipped the branching
    spruce,
And golden fingers sprouted on the pine ;
And June came in before its curls were loose,
Or laughed laburnum in the clear sunshine.

Late, late they came, but yet they came at last,
Lilac, laburnum, sweet Forget-me-not ;
But waiting for my summer, summer passed
In flowerless hoping, and in fruitless thought.

Came sunshine to the blossoms and the flowers,
Came gladness to the earth and wandering bee,
Came balmy airs and dews and tender showers,
But my spring never came, for ne'er came he.

Borland Hall, p. 146.

GLENARADALE.

THERE is no fire of the crackling boughs
  On the hearth of our fathers,
There is no lowing of brown-eyed cows
  On the green meadows,
Nor do the maidens whisper vows
  In the still gloaming,
    Glenaradale.

There is no bleating of sheep on the hill
  Where the mists linger,
There is no sound of the low hand-mill
  Ground by the women,
And the smith's hammer is lying still,
  By the brown anvil,
    Glenaradale.

Ah ! we must leave thee, and go away
  Far from Ben Luibh,
Far from the graves where we hoped to lay
  Our bones with our fathers,
Far from the kirk where we used to pray
  Lowly together,
    Glenaradale.

We are not going for hunger of wealth,
  For the gold and silver,
We are not going to seek for health
  On the flat prairies,
Nor yet for the lack of fruitful tilth
  On thy green pastures,
    Glenaradale.

Content with the croft and the hill were we,
    As all our fathers,
Content with the fish in the lake to be
    Carefully netted,
And garments spun of the wool from thee,
    O black-faced wether
        Of Glenaradale.

No father here but would give a son
    For the old country,
And his mother the sword would have girded on
    To fight her battles ;
Many's the battle that has been won
    By the brave tartans,
        Glenaradale.

But the big-horned stag and his hinds, we know,
    In the high corries,
And the salmon that swirls the pool below
    Where the stream rushes,
Are more than the hearts of men, and so
    , We leave thy green valley,
        Glenaradale.

Kildrostan, p. 153.

THE BROOK AND THE RIVER.

A STREAM from the heath-purpled mountain
    Comes, with a gush,
From the star-moss round its fountain,
    Breaking the hush
Of the silent, songless mountain.

Peewit-and-curlew-haunted,
    Foaming, it flows
There where the wild deer undaunted
    Bells, as it goes
Peewit-and-curlew-haunted.

It plays with the rowan and bracken,
    And grey lichened stone,
But never its pace will it slacken,
    Still hurrying on,
Though it plays with the rowan and bracken.

A river winds 'neath the shadows
    Of pine-wood and oak,
And hums to the bee-humming meadows,
    And the white flock
That bleats from the mists and the shadows.

Down to the still river hastens
    The swift-flowing stream,
And aye as the distance it lessens
    Its bright waters gleam,
And it leaps and sparkles and hastens,

Till in the calm-flowing river
    Softly it sinks,
And hears not and heeds not for ever
    What fern or tree thinks,
But only the low-whispering river.

O Love! my river full-flowing,
    Wait, wait for me;
O Love! my love, ever-growing,
    Hastens to thee
For rest in thy river calm-flowing.

Raban, p. 59.

BUDDING.

IT was the gloaming of the day,
  And first pale glimmer of the moon,
The fishing-boats were in the bay,
And to and fro they seemed to sway,
  Rhythmic, to a mystic tune,
  In the pale glimmer of the moon.

We sat us on a thymy bank,
  Where sea-pink and the wild-rose grew,
And blue campanulas were rank,
And wild geranium blossoms drank
  Red sunsets that enriched their hue,
  And pansies twinkled, gold and blue.

And fronting us the broad sea-sand
  Spread, ribbed and freckled, to the spray,
Crisp-curving to the curving land,
And plashing on the pebbly strand;
  Beyond, the vague, vast waters lay
  Lazily heaving in the bay.

Three children played along the beach
  With laughter, as the small waves broke;
I heard their laughter and their speech
Rippling along the sandy beach,
  Though fear and trouble in me woke
  Like the waves surging as they broke.

B

I told my love, and for a space
　She gazed out far away from me.
O throbbing heart, how still the place!
Was that a smile that lit her face?
　Or but the moon drawn from the sea
　To kiss the lips that can bless me?

I told the love you knew before;
　You said, I did not need to tell,
And that you would not answer more,
For that I also knew before
　The secret of your heart so well
　It did not need that you should tell.

Hilda, p. 88.

BURSTING.

O PATHWAY through the meadow green,
　And thou, grey stile, beneath the thorn,
　And murmurous river softly borne
In dimpling ripplets hardly seen,

Sweet path by happy footsteps worn,
　If all our visions linger there,
　The poet now shall find thine air,
More fancy-full than early morn.

We wandered in a dreamland fair,
　Beside the huge, coiled willow trees,
　Discoursing of a life to please
The Man who took our grief and care.

Not ours the dull, ignoble ease
   Of cushioned seats, or routs and balls,
   Brain-dulling dinners, civil calls,
And poor respectabilities;

Not ours to care for marble halls;
   A modest home, and frugal fare,
   With love for cobwebbed wines and rare,
And peace for pictures on the walls—

For more than these we would not care;
   But generous culture should be ours,
   And pious use of all our powers,
And knowledge, as the primal pair

Knew all the beasts and birds and flowers;
   And with our best we'd serve the Best,
   And in His goodness find our rest,
Untroubled through the years and hours.

Hilda, p. 91.

WORK AND SPIRIT.

Is it the work that makes life great and true?
   Or the true soul that, working as it can,
Does faithfully the task it has to do,
   And keepeth faith alike with God and man?

Ah! well; the work is something; the same
    gold
   Or brass is fashioned now into a coin,
Now into fairest chalice that shall hold
   To panting lips the sacramental wine:

Here the same marble forms a cattle-trough
    For brutes by the wayside to quench their
      thirst,
And there a god emerges from the rough
    Unshapely block—yet they were twins at first.

One pool of metal in the melting pot
    A sordid, or a sacred thought inspires;
And of twin marbles from the quarry brought.
    One serves the earth, one glows with altar-fires.

There's something in high purpose of the soul
    To do the highest service to its kind;
There's something in the art that can unroll
    Secrets of beauty shaping in the mind.

Yet he who takes the lower room, and tries
    To make his cattle-trough with honest heart,
And could not frame the god with gleaming
      eyes,
    As nobly plays the more ignoble part.

And maybe, as the higher light breaks in
    And shows the meaner task he has to do,
He is the greater that he strives to win
    Only the praise of being just and true.

For who can do no thing of sovran worth
    Which men shall praise, a higher task may
      find,
Plodding his dull round on the common earth,
    But conquering envies rising in the mind.

And God works in the little as the great
A perfect work, and glorious over all—
Or in the stars that choir with joy elate,
Or in the lichen spreading on the wall.

Raban, p. 21.

A WISH.

JUST a path that is sure,
  Thorny or not,
And a heart honest and pure,
Keeping the path that is sure,
  That be my lot :
Life is no merry-making,
Hark ! how the waves are breaking !

Just plain duty to know,
  Irksome or not,
And truer and better to grow
In doing the duty I know—
  That I have sought :
Life is no merry-making,
How the stiff pine trees are quaking !

Just to keep battling on,
  Weary or not,
Sure of the Right alone,
As I keep battling on,
  For the true thought :
Life is no merry-making,
Ah ! how men's hearts are breaking !

Raban, p. 52.

SCATTERED.

SCATTERED to East and West and North,
   Some with the faint heart, some the stout,
Each to the battle of life went forth,
   And all alone we must fight it out.

We had been gathered from cot and grange,
   From the moorland farm, and the terraced street,
Brought together by chances strange,
   And knit together by friendship sweet.

Not in the sunshine, not in the rain,
   Not in the night of the stars untold,
Shall we ever all meet again,
   Or be as we were in the days of old.

But as ships cross, and more cheerily go
   Having changed tidings upon the sea,
So I am richer by them, I know,
   And they are not poorer, I trust, by me.

                    Raban, p. 49.

WAITING.

WEARILY drag the lagging hours
   To him who, waiting to be hired,
   Is by enforcëd idlesse tired
More than by strain of all his powers :
   Wearily, having in his heart
   The hope to play a worthy part,
   And scorning each ignoble art.

Girt for the fight, he waits forlorn,
  And O ! it irks him sore to rest,
  And watch, too oft with mocking jest,
Things done that fill his soul with scorn,
  As he with folded hands must sit,
  While lesser men of scanty wit
  Get all the work, and tangle it.

So life grows bitter; or perhaps
  Hope flirts a moment in his face,
  Then trips off to another place,
And pours its treasures in the laps
  Of some dull souls whose easy feet
  Will tread the old familiar beat
  Contented getting much to eat.

And lo ! the work remains undone,
  And work is what he hungers for,
  But cannot find an open door,
And loiters idly in the sun,
  Still waiting with his heart on fire,
  And wasting with its great desire,
  Waiting and finding none to hire.

Raban, p. 50.

HOPE.

A LITTLE Kirk, beneath a steep green hill,
  With a grey spire that peeps o'er tall elm-trees,
In a still, pastoral land of brook and rill,
And broomy knoll, and sleepy, dripping mill,
  Far from the stir of cities and of seas:

And near the Kirk, low nestling in the copse,
  With honeysuckle clad, and roses red,
A little Manse, whose sweet-flowered garden
    slopes
Down to the river where the river drops
  With murmuring ripple o'er a pebbly bed.

How happily the days and years might flow
  Among the silent shepherds brooding long,
In pious labour, studious to know,
And patient service, till their life should grow
  From thoughtful silence into thoughtful song ;

To pass from house to house in visit free,
  Welcome as sunshine at the smoking hearth,
To take the little children on the knee,
And bless them, as He did in Galilee,
  Who came with blessing unto all the earth ;

To speak to them of Duty and of God,
  And of the Love that clasped the bitter Cross,
And of the health and comfort of His rod,
And go before them on the way He trod,
  Who found Life's glory and fulness in its loss ;

To share in all the joys and griefs they have,
  To bless the bridal, not else thought com-
    plete,
To stand beside the cradle and the grave,
And tell them how the meek and true and brave,
  Turn graves to cradles where the sleep is sweet.

O happy lot ! with one, to brighten life,
  Smiling soft-eyed beside the evening fire,
Sharing the sorrow, sweetening all the strife,
And leaning on her lord, a loving wife,
  And cherished by her lord with fond desire.

Dream of the golden gloaming of the day !
  Dream of the night beneath the folding star !
Dream of the hungry heart that in me lay !
Dream by the river rippling soft away
  Into the tremulous moonshine—which dreams
    are.

Raban, p. 57.

MORALIZING.

Roses fair on thorns do grow ;
And they tell me even so
Sorrows into virtues grow :
      Heigh-ho !
It was a stroke
Brought the stream from the flinty rock.

Frosty winter kills out weeds ;
And they tell me evil seeds
Die out in the heart that bleeds :
      Heigh-ho !
And some have faith
That dying is the death of Death.

Ah! the loss may yet be gain,
Bitter bliss may spring from pain,
As the bird-songs after rain :
       Heigh-ho !
But nought shall be
Ever again the same to me.

Raban, p. 64.

ORWELL.

I STAND on the shore of the lake,
   Where the small wave ripples and frets ;
O the land has its weeds, and the lake has its
     reeds,
   And the heart has its vain regrets.

Hark! how the skylarks sing,
   Far up about God's own feet,
And the click of the loom is in each little room,
   Of the long, bare village street.

Yonder the old home stands,
   With the little grey kirk behind ;
There are children at play on the sunny brae,
   And their shouts come down the wind,

With the smell of the old sweet flowers
   We planted there long ago ;
And the red-moss rose still buds and blows
   By the door, where it used to grow.

All of it still unchanged,
   Yet all so changed to me ;
For love then was sweet, and its bliss complete.
   And there was no cloud to see.

But the light is quenched and gone
   That brightened the place of yore.
And all the suns and the shining ones
   Shall bring back that light nevermore.

Ah me ! for the shore and the lake
   Where the small wave ripples and frets !
The land has its weeds, and the lake has its
   reeds,
   And the heart has its vain regrets.

Heretic, p. 231.

CHARACTER SKETCHES.

THOROLD.

     By the door,
Where it was hid by honey-suckle sprays
And briar-rose that trailed around the porch,
There stood a youth, at early twilight, making
Impatient gestures, switching thistle-down
And nettle and dandelion, and whate'er
His hasty strokes might reach ; yet humorous
Rather than fretful, for the art was his
To break vexations with a ready jest,
As one that, on the stirrup duly rising,
Rides lightly through the world. A graceful
   youth,
And tall, though slightly stooping, with features
   high
And thin and colourless ; yet earnest life
Beamed full of hope and energy and help
From his great lustrous eyes, though now ·and
   then
They swam into a dreamy, far-off gaze,
As seeing the invisible. He was

A student who had travelled many a field
Of arduous learning, planted venturous foot
On giddy ledge of speculative thought,
And searched for truth o'er mountain, shore, and
    sea,
In stone and flower, and every living thing
Where he might read the open secret of God
With his own eyes, and ponder out its meaning.
Intent he was to know, and knowing do
The work laid to his hand; yet evermore,
As he toiled up the solemn stair with joy,
Caught by some outlook on a larger world,
He seemed to pause, and gaze, and dream a
    dream.
These moods I noted when he was my pupil,
And some strange vocable from India,
Or fragment of the old Etrurian speech
Would suddenly arrest his eager quest,
And sunder us, like the ocean or the grave.

    .   .   .   .

Trained for a priest, for that is still the pride
And high ambition of the Scottish mother,
There was a kind of priestly purity
In him, and a deep, undertone of awe
Ran through his gayest fancies, and his heart
Reached out its sympathies, and laid fast hold
On the outcast, the unlovely and alone
I' the world. But being challenged at the door
Of God's high Temple to indue himself
With armour that he had not proved, to clothe
With articles of ready-made Belief
His Faith inquisitive, he rent the Creed
Trying to fit it on, and cast it from him;

Then took it up again, and found it worn
With age, and riddled by the moth, and rotten.
Therefore he trod it under foot, and went
Awhile with only scant fig-leaves to clothe
His naked spirit, longing after God,
But more for knowledge panting than for faith.
The Priest was left behind ; the hope of Glory
Became pursuit of Fame ; and yet ·a light
From heaven kept hovering always over him,
Like twilight from a sun that had gone down.

Olrig Grange, p. 7.

LADY ANNE DEWHURST.

LADY Anne Dewhurst on a crimson couch
Lay, with a rug of sable o'er her knees,
In a bright boudoir in Belgravia ;
Most perfectly arrayed in shapely robe
Of sumptuous satin, lit up here and there
With scarlet touches, and with costly lace,
Nice-fingered maidens knotted in Brabant :
And all around her spread magnificence
Of bronzes, Sèvres vases, marquetrie,
Rare buhl, and bric-à-brac of every kind
From Rome and Paris and the centuries
Of far-off beauty. All of goodly colour,
Or graceful form that could delight the eye,
In orderly disorder lay around,
And flowers with perfume scented the warm·air.

Stately and large and beautiful was she
Spite of her sixty summers, with an eye

Trained to soft languors, that could also flash,
Keen as a sword and sharp—a black bright eye,
Deep sunk beneath an arch of jet. She had
A weary look, and yet the weariness
Seemed not so native as the worldliness
Which blended with it. Weary and worldly, she
Had quite resigned herself to misery
In this sad vale of tears, but fully meant
To nurse her sorrow in a sumptuous fashion,
And make it an expensive luxury ;
For nothing she esteemed that nothing cost.

Beside her, on a table round, inlaid
With precious stones by Roman art designed,
Lay phials, scents, a novel and a Bible,
A pill box, and a wine glass, and a book
On the Apocalypse ; for she was much
Addicted unto physic and religion,
And her physician had prescribed for her
Jellies and wines and cheerful Literature.
The book on the Apocalypse was writ
By her chosen pastor, and she took the novel
With the dry sherry, and the pills prescribed.
A gorgeous, pious, comfortable life
Of misery she lived; and all the sins
Of all her house, and all the nation's sins,
And all shortcomings of the Church and State,
And all the sins of all the world beside,
Bore as her special cross, confessing them
Vicariously day by day, and then
She comforted her heart, which needed it,
With bric-à-brac and jelly and old wine.

Olrig Grange, p. 69.

SQUIRE DEWHURST.

A GREY old man sat in that dim grey room,
Wrapt in a dressing-gown of soft grey stuff,
And puzzling o'er a paper wearily
Of circles, squares and pentagons, and lines
Of logarithms, he strove to disentangle.
He was a little, brisk, bald-headed man,
With fiery eyes, and forehead narrow and high
And far-retiring : one who could have led
A regiment to the belching cannon's mouth
If wisely ordered when ; or might have headed
The cheery hunt across the stubble field,
Taking the fences gallantly, nor turning
From the wide brook to seek the safer ford.
But being held in London half the year,
And with no taste for politics or fashion,
Or such religion as he came across,
He took to Science, made experiments,
Bought many nice and costly instruments,
Heard lectures, and believed he understood
Beetle-browed Science wrestling with the fact
To find its meaning clear ; but all in vain.
He thought he thought, and yet he did not think,
But only echoed still the common thought,
As might an empty room. The forehead high
And fiery eye had no reflection in them
To brood and hatch the secret of the world.
He could but skim and dip, like restless swallow
Fly-catching on the surface of all knowledge
Anthropologic and Botanical
And Chemical, and what was last set forth

By charlatan to stun the vulgar sense.
But yet a strain of noble chivalry
Ran through his nature, and a faint crisp humour
Rippled his thought, and would have been a joy
Had life been kindlier ; but like forming dew
Seized in the night, and chilled into the spikes
And crystals of the hoar-frost, so the play
And mirth of genial nature had been changed
Into sharp prickles ; and his cheeriest smile
Verged on a sneer, and ran to mocking laughter.
Yet under all his pottering at Science,
And deeper than his feeble cynic sneer,
Lay a great love, to which he fondly clung,
For Rose, the stately daughter of his house.

Olrig Grange, p. 104

DICK DALGLEISH.

JUST a mechanic with big, broad head,—
  Carpenter, maybe, or engineer,—
Deft with a skilled hand at winning his bread,
  Scornful of varnish and show and veneer ;
Rough-handed, plain-spoken, strong in his youth,
  Loyal to all of his order and craft :
Loudly maintaining the fact and the truth,
  At all pretences as loudly he laughed ;
Laughed at quill-drivers, and white-fingered dandies
  Measuring ribbons with yard-stick and tape ;
Laughed more at frowsy men doctoring brandies,
  And calling their drugs the pure fruit of the
    grape :

C

He slept through the night, and he toiled all the
    day,
And nothing he drunk but the brook by the way.

Out on a holiday, wholesomely dressed,
    Clean-washed, clean-shirted, his wife by his side,
With a small baby she clasped to her breast,
    And chirped to, and watched with a motherly
       pride.
Proud of her baby, and proud of her Man,
    All her young face was like sunshine to see;
No sickly vapours had she, nor a wan
    Fine-lady look, but was healthful as he.
How she looked up to him! Who was so clever?
    Who was so good as her Dick? It is true,
He was blunt-spoken, but then he would never
    Harm a poor worm or a fly, if he knew;
And he read everything—science, and plays,
And poems, and all that the newspaper says.

Out on a holiday, sailing down
    The broad clear river that bore away
Thronging crowds from the broiling town
    To the birch-clad hill or the sandy bay;
Shrewdly he glanced at either shore
    Lined with the half-finished skeleton ships,
Spoke of their rigging abaft and afore,
    And what they might do at their trial trips;
Plainly knew all about this one's gearing,
    The other one's engines, paddles, or screw,
And the new methods of working and steering,
    What coal they needed, and what coal could do;
And shrewdly projected a wonderful dream,
    Into the future, of iron and steam.

I scarce know why, but I rather took
  To the manly bearing of him, and the fond
Young pride which his wife showed in every look
  Than to all the rest, as their ways I conned :
They were mostly broad-cloth citizen folks,
  Each with his newspaper where he read
The markets first, and the price of stocks,
  And what at the bankrupt sittings was said :
They carried their business with them always,
  While their wives were towny and overdressed,
Talked of their city life, and its small ways,
  And dinners and weddings and fashion and taste.
So I took my seat, with a frank good-day,
By the big mechanic in homespun grey.

I was fain to speak of his craft and trade,
  But he went rather at first for books :
Did I not think that Darwin made
  A case for the worms as against the rooks ?
What had the birds done for earth like these
  Dumb, silent ploughers who made the soil
For rooks to nestle on its high trees,
  And man to live by his sweat and toil ?
That was a man, sir, with hardly a rival
  For his power to see, and his grasp of thought ;
And as for his doctrine of fit survival,
  That's the new gospel this age has got ;
And we must be rid of the drones in the hive,
That the real workers may live and thrive.

They're nearly all drones now on board here
    to-day ;
  Our lads went off with an earlier boat ;
But wife, sir, and baby must have their own way,

And she likes the gentle folks when she's afloat.
It is so, you know, Kate; you're fain now to hear
  The sweet-spoken damsels come praising your
    child;
And if we went down, you would rather appear
  With respectable folk, pretty-mannered and mild,
Than stand at the judgment with Dick, Tom, and
    Harry
  Not more than half-sobered with gulps of the
    sea—
Oh, how can I say so when you chose to marry
  Such a blunt working chap, such a rough tyke
    as me?
That's true; yet you cannot deny it was you
Brought me here with this soft-handed, soft-headed
    crew.

Would you wish me, old girl, now, to be just like
    these,
  With broad cloth and white linen worn every
    day,
And to saunter through 'Change for an hour at
    my ease,
  And call that my work, though it looks so like
    play?
Their brow never sweats with the work they have
    done,
  Unless at some queer job that looks rather ill,
And then it is but for the risk that they run,
  When they shuffle the cards for a trial of skill.
Now, I come home at evening, Kate, dirty and
    weary,
  But my conscience is clean, and my head too,
    is clear;

I don't sit and drink wine, and make the house
    dreary,
  As some of them do half the days of the year;
I take on no stains from my work or my play,
Which a pail of fresh water will not wash away.

They buy and they sell for the rise or fall,
  When neither a rise nor a fall should be,
Filching a profit still, great or small,
  For the doing of nothing that I can see.
There's a little chap sitting yonder—look !
  He's bulling and bearing all the day long ;
And they're fain to glance at his jotting book,
  For they say that his guesses are seldom
    wrong;
I call him the big flea blood-sucking commerce,
  And these are the little fleas blood-sucking him;
And they live upon us, all our winters and
    summers—
  Swarms of them, sir—in the handsomest trim,
They make their game and the stakes are laid,
And they rake in the gold which the workers
    made.

Yet what have they done for the world by their
   strokes
  Of betting and hedging? I want to know that.
And who is the happier hearing their jokes ?
  And whose life is helped by the jobs they are at?
With their sharp arithmetic they fashion a blade
  That cuts a big slice of our profit away ;
And yet they've done nothing for it except trade
  On the folly of some, for which all have to pay !

I used to read Carlyle, and laughed at his "gig-
        men,"
    And I still like the old fellow's rough tongue a
        bit ;
But he never yet said how the "clothes-men"
        and "wig-men"
    Must make way at last for the men who are fit.
That's Darwin's discovery ; and how can you doubt
These chaps, like the Dodo, are bound to die out?

When you spoke to me first, you were wishing
        to know
    About us, the working men ; what our thoughts
        are ;
And whereto our strikes and our unions grow ;
    And how near the end is, or, maybe, how far.—
Ah, folks are grown curious about us, who once
    Sniffed the grease of our moleskins, and hurried
        them past.
You're not of that sort, I allow ; and perchance
    We 'are crustier, now that our day's come at
        last,
Than we should be. That comes of the way we've
        been living ;
    Men trample on man, and they make him a brute ;
Though of course we ought all to be taking and
        giving,
    And keep our good humour and manhood to
        boot.
But those who have tasted of slight and neglect,
When folk grow too civil, are apt to suspect.

I don't say it's right. But at one time I made
    What was plainly to me a new thing in our line ;

A saving of labour to quicken the trade,
  And bring in more wealth than the gold in a
    mine.
Well, I spoke to the head of our firm; but he
    turned,
  With a big oath, and bade me go work at my
    tools ;
He had heard such tales once till his fingers were
    burned,
  And he found that your workmen-inventors
    were fools.
But afterwards, learning more truly about it,
  Oh, he spoke me so bland, and would fain see
    the thing ;
So I brought forth my model—as proud, do not
    doubt it,
  As Kate of her baby there,—and with a swing
Of the big hammer, I dashed it in bits,
Saying, What could come out of a working-man's
    wits ?

I had toiled at it, sir, every night for a year,
  So hopeful and happy in seeing my thought
Turned now into iron, and coming out clear,
  At last, through a plain inspiration I got.—
For why should not God inspire minds to invent
  As well as to preach, and be praised for His
    gift ?
Sir, it came like a flash and a thrill that were
    sent
  In a moment of failure, when I was adrift ;
As "the still small voice," which the prophet
    must hearken,
  Because it was God's, so the thing came to me,

Like the gladness of light when that failure did
    darken
    Around me, and I was as broken as he:
And what is the joy of their gold and their gain,
To the gladness I had when I saw it all plain?

You think it was childish to waste the ripe fruit
    Of my labour and thought. Not a whit; it's
    all here
As clear in my head as that day, and to boot
    Some riper thought still that may some time
    appear.
But I told you this only to show how, in vain,
    Folk think all at once they can heal the huge
    rent
In our social order where one's heart and brain
    Find seldom the right place for which they were
    meant.—
But why don't I patent the thing I invented?—
    Oh, and rise in the world, as they say, and
    grow rich,
And have a grand house finely papered and
    painted,
    And mount me a-horseback to land in a ditch,
And dress my good Kate in her sealskin and silk,
And quaff my champagne as it were bottled
    milk?

Well, I once knew a man with a head-piece to
    think,
    And hands that could work out the thought of
    his head—
It is true that he had a bad weakness for drink,

And would whimper about it, and wish he
  were dead ;—
But he took to that line, and had everything fine,
  A house in a big square, with lamps at the
  door,
And carriages, horses, and flunkies, and wine,
  And heaven knows what that he had not before.
But the ladies were shy of his wife ; and the
  flunkies—
  The lazy fat rogues, I'd have sweated them
  well—
At the back of his chair stood, and grinned there
  like monkeys,
  And down in the kitchen they laughed at his
  bell ;
And he had not a moment of comfort or peace,
Till a crash stript him bare as a sheep of its
  fleece.

No, I'll not take that way, sir ; I don't care to
  rise
  Above my own class—we are happier so.
The Son of the Carpenter now, He was wise
  In the old town of Nazareth long, long ago.
We are not very pious, we workmen, I fear,
  Don't go much to church, but we read about
  Him ;
And the things that we read are not quite what
  we hear
  The minister blow off like froth from the brim
Of a pot of small beer. Nay, I don't blame the
  preacher ;
  It's just what we want that we find in our
  books ;

As the sun is a painter to some, and a bleacher
  To others; it is as the eye is that looks;
You open the door to which you have the key,
And I find the message that God meant for me.

But the Carpenter, now, did not care to be great,
  And to ape what the fine Lords of Herod
    might do,
Nor yet be called Rabbi, and sit in the gate
  As a Judge, or a Parliament man to the Jew.
The fox had his hole, and the bird of the air
  Had its nest; but He had not a roof o'er His
    head,
And heeded not purple and sumptuous fare,
  And borrowed a grave when He lay with the
    dead.
And this is the gospel I read in the story—
  Though I don't say it mayn't have another to
    you—
The Lord did not seek His own honour and glory,
  But stood by His craftsmen and fishers all
    through.
He held to His class that their ills He might cure
And lift up the head of the needy and poor.

Well, that is our gospel too, that is our Ark,
  Not to rise from our class, but to raise the
    class higher,
Not to take to the nice ways of lawyer or clerk,
  Not to turn from the hammer, the file, and the
    fire;
But to stand by our order, and stick to our tools,
  And still win our bread by the sweat of our brow

And to organise labour by Christian-like rules,
  Not that some, but that all may be better than
    now,
May have homes of more comfort, and lives with
    more leisure
To read, and to think, and to well understand,
And to get, like us here now, some holiday
    pleasure ;
  For they do the work that enriches the land.
No ! I don't care to rise for myself, till I see
The rest get a chance, too, of rising with me.

You're a Christian, sir? So am I, in a way,
  Though some of our fellows, and good fellows
    too,
Have no other gospel or God, as they say,
  Than Man, and what man's brain and fingers
    may do.
I don't go with them, but I reckon my trade
  May be my church too, if the right heart is
    there,
A-healing the wounds which the selfish have
    made,
  And helping the helpless their burden to
    bear,
He is parson and priest, though his apron be
    leather,
  And he tuck up his shirt sleeves to do his job
    well,
Whose heart is most loving to sister and brother.
  Most ready to go where the sorrowful dwell,
And to show to the erring the right way of
    truth,
And bring them again to the faith of their youth.

Now, the faith of my youth was that Christ
        would redeem
    The life of the poor from its sorrow and sin,
Would wake up the world from its wealth-loving
        dream
    To seek the true riches of manhood within,
In wisdom and worth, and the peace which they
        bring.
    That's the word which I heard from my old
        mother's lips ;
But now its another guess-song that they sing,
    And the light of her heaven has all suffered
        eclipse.
Oh, we boast that the poor man may rise in the
        world,
    And we point to his sons who are lords in the
        state,
A-driving in carriages, scented and curled,
    Or making their bow to the gold-stick-in-wait.
And where shall you find, now, a sight so grand,
Except in this truth-loving, Christ-serving land?

Well, well ! what rare tricks we do play, to be
        sure,
    With our conjuring cards, and our thimbles
        and peas !
To think that a God could come here, and endure
    A cross to make lordlings and ladies like these,
And to leave all the rest of His brothers to
        pine !
    There's your thimble, and Christ in't ; but
        presto ! begone !
Lo ! the devil is there, where the glory divine
    A short while ago sat in sorrow alone !

O blessed the poor—if they only get money ;
  And blessed the meek—if they stand to their
    rights ;
And all who are selfish shall have milk and
  honey,
  For they are the salt of the world and its
    lights !
Ay ! that's the new gospel, I call it, of Gold ;
But we working men will hold fast to the old.

Yes, I know we're divided, as other folk are,
  And what is yet worse, we are cursed with that
    drink ;
And many are selfish, and some of us mar
  A good cause with bad ways, and some do not
    think ;
And we've blundered, 'tis true, and been wrong
  now and then,
  And done what we should not—as who has not
    done ?
But we'll learn by our failures ; we're only poor
  men,
  Kept like children till lately, now trying to
    run ;
And sometimes, of course, we get tript up and
  tumble ;
  But still on our clouds, lo ! the rainbow is
    set,
And a light springeth up in the hearts of the
  humble,
  Will grow to more fulness, and gladden us
    yet—
But there ! I've been preaching until I have got
A drop in my heart that is bitter and hot.

That's the way with all preaching ; it don't make
   one sweet.
   Where's Kate and the baby? They'll put me
   all right.
Oh, the ladies are praising its hands and its feet
   And its mouth and its nose, and its precious
   eyesight !
Well, well ! do you see, sir, that narrow green
   glen,
   With the strip of dark alders that show where
   the stream
Flows on in its loneliness far from men,
   And ripples, and murmurs like one in a dream?
I speak like a fool, for of course you can't hear it,
   Though I hear it singing away to itself,
Or sobbing at times like a sore troubled spirit,
   Or laughing perhaps as it slides down a shelf;
I was born there, sir ; and we're going to try
A week with old mother—Kate and baby and I.

North Country Folk, p. 53.

AMORY HILL.

I.

Does any one know about Amory Hill?
   What an unrestful mind she had,
   Questioning everything, good and bad,
Subtle in thought, and firm of will !
   Beautiful, too, in her way : but what
   Ever could come of a girl like that?

Oh, you remember the large grey eyes ;
　　What a keen look in them did lie,
　　Fain to be told the reason why
We ever held anything true or wise !
　　And say what you might, she would still find out,
　　Somehow or other, a ground for doubt.

Under the Word she must see the Thing,
　　Never content with the neatest phrase ;
　　The coin might be of the ancient days,
But still she must try if it truly ring,
　　And bite it too with her dainty teeth,
　　For it might look well, and be false beneath.

No matter how old a lie might be,
　　Age, she said, could not make it true ;
　　No matter though truth be fresh and new,
It was the pleasanter sight to see,
　　Like a fresh star your eyes behold,
　　Where never a star had been seen of old.

Liked ! how could she be liked, a girl
　　Who'd squat her down in a quiet nook,
　　Out of the way, with a folio book,
With all the rest of us there in a whirl
　　Of work or talk ? And she did not heed,
　　If only we left her at peace to read.

Of course, her doubts and her questions tried
　　Every one's patience, more or less,
　　And the older folk, when they felt the stress,
Were fain their ignorance to hide,
　　And sent her off, with a sharp rebuke,
　　Back again to her folio book.

Somehow she never took it ill,
  Whatsoever you chanced to say ;
  But not in the least did it change her way;
She soon had another question still :
  Never the same one twice, for now
  She would puzzle it out by herself somehow.

What could come of a girl like that,
  Who would not walk on the common road,
  Who fretted at bearing the common load,
And did not know what she would be at,
  And was not sure of the common creed,
  And gave not her dress a moment's heed?

Oh, Amory Hill! Amory Hill!
  And yet how good she was and nice,
  Scorning a meanness, and hating a vice,
With a brave true heart and a patient will,
  Loving the truth, and not afraid !—
  What has come of the grey-eyed maid?

AMORY HILL.

II.

I THOUGHT you had heard of Amory Hill :
  It made at the time a mighty stir,
  But nobody now-a-days thinks of her.
We wonder at nothing, good or ill,
  After two or three days are past—
  That is enough for a comet to last.

Amory grew, as you might expect,
  From a doubting, questioning, restless elf
  To a woman who brooded by herself
About the Church, and the Lord's Elect,
  About the fate of the quick and dead,
  Doubting the more, the more she read.

At a Revival some one got
  A hold of her for a little while ;
  And she sang their hymns with an angel's smile,
And tried to live on their shallow thought ;
  But back the questions came, and then
  Oh, she was deep in her doubts again.

She writ a book that I tried to read,
  But could not tell what it was about—
  Just like thoughts that she had thrown out
Into the darkness of thought and deed,
  And heard them in the silence roll
  Back again on her yearning soul.

Poor girl ! she wandered, here and there,
  From pastures green where the grace was rife,
  Seeking the Way and the Truth and the Life,
And finding but shadows and dim despair,
  Till she came to the perilous brink of Faith,
  Beyond which lieth the realm of death.

Star after star had all gone out,
  Darkest night was on all her sky ;
  And moaning as one who is ready to die,
Ah, me ! she said, Must I live without
  God and his Christ and the hope divine,
  That erewhile gladdened this life of mine?

D

Then one laid hold of her, drew her back
    From the dismal gloom of that deadly brink,
    Told her that now she must cease to think,
And then no wisdom her soul should lack;
    If to the Church she would only bow,
    It would do all of her thinking now.

Bland his speech was, and mild his look;
    Was he an angel come from heaven
    To save the soul that was tempest-driven
There where in terror and pain it shook?
    And what had all of her thinking brought,
    Except despair of all certain thought?

So straightway into his arms she fell,
    Cast away Reason, and swallowed the Creeds,
    Mumbled her Aves, and counted her beads,
And said it was good in peace to dwell
    With Nuns who had not a thought in their
        head—
    But is it the peace of the living or dead?

She does much good to the sick and poor,
    Going about in that quaint odd dress
    With the little book which her fingers press:
But then she did quite as much good before,
    For Amory Hill was always sweet,
    And came like a sunbeam along the street.

AMORY HILL.

III.

WHO would know me for Amory Hill,
  Once the plague and the tease of School,
  Querying lesson, and breaking rule?
And yet I fear I am Amory still,
  Under the white cap and the hood
  Of the patient merciful Sisterhood.

I've tried, till I think there is no use trying
  To be anything other than I was made;
  I've sought the light, and I've sought the shade,
I've crushed my thought, when it rose defying,
  I've nursed submission, and fondled pain,
  Yet ever the thoughts come back again.

Weary, I'm weary; what shall I do?
  Oh, will that chatter of theirs not cease?
  Here I had hoped to have quiet peace,
In the daily round of duties true,
  And the tranquil hymn, and the whispered
    prayer,
  Freed from the burden of trouble and care.

Once I wrestled, in earnest thought,
  With weighty problems of truth and faith,
  With the high issues of life and death,
And what we should not do, what we ought:
  But here our wrestle is not to think—
  Can it be more sinful to see than wink?

Does God, indeed, mean that we should not bear
The burden of thought? or fashion a life
Of peace, instead of the noble strife
Inspiring ever the soul to dare,
And make fresh conquests, if it may,
On the realm of darkness, day by day?

Oh! but this is rebellion, this is sin:
So they tell me, and I have tried
To crush it out, and have done, beside,
Many a penance for letting it in.
But is it sinful? and can it be right
To close the shutters, when God is Light?

This is the hour when they sit and talk,
Oh, such nothings! and not without
Touches of malice too, all about
What they saw in the daily walk
To visit the sick and the poor, when they
Looked on the world and its wicked way.

But why is the world more wicked than they?
They were silly girls ere they took the vow,
And they're just as silly sisters now.
Ribbons and gawds may be put away,
And love and marriage be counted shame,
Yet heart and mind may be still the same.

How should they differ from what they were?—
Hear! how they chatter as school girls do,
And gossip about the folk they knew,   ·
And who was married, and who was there:—
I blame them not, if they did not blame
The world as wicked for doing the same.

Are all the people who try to do good
  As little-minded as those I've known ?
  Ere I came here, how I used to groan
At Dorcas meetings in angry mood !
  And the District Visitors need, I'm sure,
  Quite as much visiting as the poor.

Oh, how I shrank from the vulgar talk,
  The fuss, and the hard mechanical way
  Of saving so many souls a day
By dropping tracts in a morning walk !
  Not so, I said, would the work be done
  Here by the consecrated Nun.

But here or there, it is all the same,
  The talk alike, and the fuss and fret,
  And the vulgar methods of clearing debt,
And the mechanical ways and lame
  For doing of spiritual work, without
The faintest thought what you are about.

And then this drilling of hands and lips !
  So many hours of work a day,
  So many hours to praise and pray,
All of our time cut into snips,
  And just as you get your mind in swing,
  There goes the bell with its ting, ting, ting !

Was I mistaken in coming here?
  Was it a hasty step I made?
  I am still free to go back, 'tis said ;
And I was not meant for a Nun, I fear.
  But they are all pleased with their happy lot,
  And what would they think if they knew my
    thought ?

It's nonsense what people were wont to say
  About the misery vows may bring,
  About the hearts that are suffering,
And the glad bright youth as it wastes away ;
  There is nothing to waste, for they have no mind
  Nor heart nor passion of any kind.

And yet I feel that I am not free.
  Oh, the subtle threads that are wound
  About us here till our souls are bound,
And there's nothing for it but just to be
  As silly as all the rest, and make
  A merit of it for Jesus' sake.

I gave up my former life in dread
  Of the rush of thoughts into my soul,
  Terrible as the waves that roll
Over the weary swimmer's head ;
  But now if I leave this, it will be
  In scorn of its dull vacuity.

Ay, if I leave it ! but dare I go?
  Do I not know what would be said?
  Better it were to be lying dead
Than pine away with a poison slow
  Of lies that would tingle in every vein,
  And break the heart with a nameless pain !

Ah ! rebel nature could not endure
  The vacant mind and the weary day,
  The effort to keep all thought away,
But for the work 'mong the sick and poor :
  It is among them that I find my good,—
  If they would not pain me by gratitude.

                          North Country Folk, p. 198.

MISS BELLA JAPP.

TO HER YOUNG MINISTER.

SPEAK out, speak out !
We are all hungering, sir, for truthful words
    Of faith or doubt ;
And we are weary of all mocking-birds
    Who would be dumb
If they might eat their meat, and do no more ;
    And only come,
And sing again what we have heard before,
And grind again the same tune at the door
    To get their crumb.

    Oh yes, yes, yes !
We have much talk, we have abundant speech
    In Rhetoric dress—
Thin thready talk that has no truth to teach ;
    Poor echoes sent
From rock-like brains that barren are of thought :
    No nutriment
On which a soul may live is to be got
From echoes which are shadows, and give not
    The least content.

    Just speak out that
Which God gives you to live on day by day ;
    And say not what
The people round about would have you say—
    Oh I could preach,

If they would let me, if I had a sphere !—
    If you would reach
The heart of others, listen first and hear
What your own heart is saying, and speak it clear
    To all and each.

    Take not your words
From pulpit, platform, or from parliament ;
    Just take the Lord's—
The words which from His lips to you are sent,
    Which few desire,
But all believe whether they will or no :
    And for no hire
Proclaim them from the housetops where you go,
And cry aloud because they burn and glow
    In you like fire !

    What ! man, you talk
Of living by the gospel you proclaim !
    Well, if you walk
So as to glorify the Lord's great name,
    You shall have meat
Enough—the meat He gave to His own Son,
    And that was sweet.
"Not muzzle the ox !" what harm that text has done,
Just making lazy "nowt" of many a one
    For meat to eat !

    I've gone to Kirk
Sixty years now since first with Jenny, nurse ;
    And what a work
I've heard them make about the Fall and Curse,
    Imputed sin,

Imputed right, imputed everything,
  Meanwhile within,
The Devil who had us in his grips would sing,
"Impute away! that's just the way to bring
  My bairns in."

  Now don't you spin
Notions and crotchet-things like that about
  Imputed sin,
When sin's a fact whereof there is no doubt;
  As you can see
Flaunting at every corner its disgrace
  Or misery,
And in the "Publics" running a hot race,
Ay! and at Kirk too smirking in the face
  O' the Pharisee.

  Then speak out, man;
Out with it plain, the Devil is in the town,
  And what we can,
That, with God's help, we must, to put him down:
  Oh, fools may scoff,
But he laughs last who truth has on his side:
  Hell's not far off
Where dead folk are; it's at your very side,
And souls drop in as balls are made to slide,
  I' th' holes at golf.

  There are the holes,
And here's the Devil's game, and well he plays;
  For thoughtless souls
Come dropping in, with some bit pleasant phrase,
  Each hour o' the day.

An easy job he's had this many a year,
    For it's poor play
We've had against him; God's been ill served here,
And it's been like to drive me mad to hear
    Their feckless way.

    But you have come
Fresh and hot-hearted, as I hear, from College,
    Freighted like some
Others, no doubt, with tons of useless knowledge.
    But O my man,
It's not your metaphysics that we need,
    Watery and wan;
Just take the Book, and with your own eyes read,
And drop the spectacles of an old-world creed
    About "The Plan."

    And preach right out
And pray; I do not mean to stamp the floor,
    And sweat and shout;
God is not deaf that you should need to roar:
    But take our sin
Right by the throat, and call it by its name,
    Nor mind the din
The Devil will raise because ye spoil his game,
Or Pharisee because he's put to shame,
    Turned outside in.

    Pick ye no words
To tickle itching ears with rhetoric;
    They have the birds
To sing to them if that is what they seek:
    Its dainty phrase

And mincing speech have been our very death
    These many days,
As in the Kirk we sought not truth and faith,
But tricks of art to hear with bated breath,
    Like fine stage plays.

    Be strong and true ;
Hold up our sins that we may see them bare,
    And hold up too
The Cross both to believe it, and to share
    Its pain and loss,
Should sorrow fill our cup unto the brim ;
    For on the Cross
We see the glory as the eye grows dim,
Only we're fain to hand it on to Him,
    Who clasped it close.

    Believing much
The Cross, that it is all our help and hope,
    We will not touch
It with our finger, fain to let it drop ;
    And therewith cease
The grace and bliss and riches that it brings,
    And all increase ;
Meanwhile we sing about the angels' wings,
And soothe the sickly conscience as it stings,
    And call this Peace.

North Country Folk, p. 210.

THE BISHOP.

God made him beautiful, to be
Drawn to all beauty tenderly,
And conscious of all beauty, whether
In things of earth or heaven or neither;
    So to rude men he seemed
    Often as one that dreamed.

But true it was that, in his soul,
The needle pointed to the pole,
Yet trembled as it pointed, still
Conscious alike of good and ill;
    In his infirmity
    Looking, O Lord, to thee.

Beautiful spirit! fallen, alas,
On times when little beauty was;
Still seeking peace amid the strife,
Still working, weary of thy life,
    Toiling in holy love,
    Panting for heaven above:

I mark thee, in an evil day,
Alone upon a lonely way;
More sad-companionless thy fate,
Thy heart more truly desolate,
    Than even the misty glen
    Of persecuted men.

For none so lone on earth as he
Whose way of thought is high and free,

Beyond the mist, beyond the cloud,
Beyond the clamour of the crowd,
    Moving, where Jesus trod,
    In the lone walk with God.

                  The Bishop's Walk. p. 16.

CONTRASTS.

TWAIN are they, sundered each from each,
    Though oft together they are brought;
Discoursing in a common speech,
    Yet having scarce a common thought;
The same sun warmed them all their days,
    They breathe one air of life serene ;
Yet, moving on their several ways,
    They walk with a whole world between.

I think they never meet without
    Some sharp encounter of their wits ;
And neither hints a faith or doubt,
    The other does not take to bits ;
For what the one regards with awe,
    The other holds a creed outworn ;
And what this boasts as perfect law,
    That turns to laughter with his scorn.

No envious grudge is in their hearts,
    Detracting from the honour due
To nobler worth, or greater parts,
    Or larger grasp, or clearer view :

Simply there is a gulf between
   Their ways of life, and modes of thought,
And nothing is by either seen
   But as the other likes it not.

With vision keen and thought complete
   Cool-headed Warham holds his way,
And all that lies about his feet
   He makes it his, and clear as day ;
All common things of natural birth
   He sets forth in a novel sense ;
But never leaves the common earth
   To seek the dim Omnipotence.

He gathers knowledge hour by hour,
   Forgetting nought that once he knew,
And handling it with conscious power
   As matter certified and true ;
And all he knows gives added might
   That still with harder thought combines ;
We wonder at the shining light,
   He wonders less the more it shines !

He has slight pity for our pain,
   For weakness, he has none at all !
He is not proud, he is not vain ;
   He is not either great or small ;
But he is strong and hard and clear
   As is a frosty winter day,
And never sheds an idle tear,
   Nor flings an idle word away.

He cannot breathe but in the breath
　Of certainty and knowledge clear ;
And where we have to walk by Faith
　He will not go, or will not fear
To search into the mysteries,
　And bid the haunting shadows go ;
And yet, with all he knows and sees,
　True wisdom somehow does not grow.

But Cromer is of finer make,
　And doth with subtler thoughts commune—
Thoughts singing oft in dim daybreak,
　And silent oft in blaze of noon ;
He sees the process Warham saw,
　But to the Power he is not blind,
Beholds the working of the Law,
　And bows to that which lies behind.

Seeking what knife can ne'er dissect,
　Nor flame-wrapt blowpipe can set free,
Nor chemic test can e'er detect,
　But only kindred mind can see,
He finds in everything a light
　Which, shunning finest power of sense,
Does more to make a man of might
　Than knowledge of the Why or Whence.

And much he knows, and much he thinks,
　But he *is* more than all he knows ;
For still aspiring, still he drinks
　Fresh inspiration as he goes,

More careful that the man should grow
  Than that the mind should understand :
He loves all creatures here below,
  And touches all with tender hand.

He pities all the pained and weak,
  And feels for their unhappy fate ;
Simple and true and brave and meek,
  He does not know that he is great ;
He looks to heaven with wondering gaze,
  And earth with awe by him is trod ;
We marvel at the words he says,
  He, at the silences of God.

Thus on their several ways they go,
  And neither other comprehends,
Yet it was God that made them so,
  And they do serve His several ends ;
That seeks for light to walk in it,
  And this for God to live in Him ;
One questions with a searching wit,
  The other trusts where all is dim.

Why quarrel with their several parts,
  Where each is good if one is best?
And who shall say that this departs,
  Restful, unto Eternal rest,
While he who loves the light goes down
  Into the darkness of the night?—
Life grows unto its perfect crown,
  And light unto a larger light.

Hilda, p. 20.

A SCHOOL-MISTRESS.

OLD Prinkle I took for a prude,
  With her hands in her black thread-mits,
Chap-fingered, and painfully good,
  Yet half-scared out of her wits ;
And at first I could not make out
What troubled a soul so devout.

'Twas not the mere burden of care
  For a score of commonplace girls,
Whose manners and dresses and hair,
  Their finger-nails, teeth, and their curls,
With their morals and dinners and laughter,
'Twas her calling in life to look after.

But parents and guardians then wanted,
  For girls at a "Finishing School,"
The old wine of Faith well decanted
  Into flasks which must also be full
Of the world, and of woman's ambition
To better her single condition.

So she had to be worldly-wise,
  And train us for "marrying well";
And she had to put on a disguise,
  And warn us of Death, too, and Hell ;
For the earthly young soul must be given
At least a top-dressing of Heaven.

E

'Twas against the grain, I admit,
   For she'd fain have been honest and true ;
She had neither much culture nor wit,
   She was simply a woman that knew
About womanly ways and things,
Such as colours and dresses and rings.

A good soul, kindly and just,
   But timid, and living in ways
She would never have chosen, but must,
   If she meant to live out all her days
In the highly respectable station
Of finishing sound education.

Not a person to train the young mind,
   For she was not at all intellectual,
And oft her religion would find
   All its efforts were quite ineffectual
To fix her stray thoughts on devotion,
Or show the least touch of emotion.

Thus, when sermon was over at noon
   On Sunday, she'd question us on it ;
But her speech would wander off soon
   To a ribbon, a gown, or a bonnet—
Or anything pretty or new
She had seen in the minister's pew.

She used to bubble and bell
   About lady-like manners and ways
In soft purling accents that well
   Suggested her own brighter days ;
Then sighed and looked timid about,
As if sure that she should be found out.

And the terror that haunted her so
　Was fear of the Governess, Lane,
Who was dismal and dreary as snow
　When it thaws in a drizzle of rain,
And sharp-eyed, and wanted the school,
And held our dear Prinkle a fool.

Lane had laws for all that we did,
　And for every hour of the day ;
This and that we were strictly forbid,
　So and so we were always to say ;
And we lived, like nuns in their cells,
'Mid an hourly ringing of bells.

We never did any great wrong,
　Such as schoolboys would do on a hint ;
And therefore she had to be strong
　On the tithing of anise and mint ;
And taught us to wet our hard pillows
At the lightest of light peccadilloes.

O the old-maiden morals we had,
　So scrupulous, prim, and demure !
What the decalogue never forbade
　Our consciences could not endure :
But life was so low-pitched and sad,
It was quite a relief to be bad.

Then, the wearisome lessons !—the proper,
　Dull prose that we read every day,
Which felt as if boiled in a copper
　To take all the flavour away !
The colourless paragraphs writ
Without reason or fancy or wit !

Yet the poems were worse; they were so
   Lack-a-daisical pretty-sublime,
Spurting upward in little jets d'eau
   To fall with a musical chime;
And we mouthed the sweet verses, Good heavens!
How we mouthed, all at sixes and sevens!

Then the darning and hemming and stitching,
   The broidery and the brocade,
The Berlin-wool figures bewitching,
   And the wonderful trees that we made,
Like green triangles in bloom
Stuck hard on the stick of a broom!

And the scales that we practised for hours,
   Till we hated the sight of the keys!
And the evenings when, ranged out like flowers,
   We had our æsthetical teas,
With music, charades, and advices,
While the parents had sherry and ices!

French was taught by a starved refugee
   Who had hurled at all tyrants defiance;
And a student, who stormed like the sea,
   Administered globules of science
Well wrapt up in texts to make sure
That the bane should have always its cure.

And thus we were "finished" at last
   On principles strictly religious,
Made ready "to come out" and cast
   Our lines in the ocean prodigious;
And begin the true business of life,
To find some one in want of a wife.

I do not blame Prinkle the least—
   She did what they asked her to do ;
They did not wish knowledge increased
   Of the wise and the right and the true ;
But they would have a gloss of devotion
On girls who had not a notion,

Except just to marry and dress,
   And to see to their cooks and their dinners,
And live on in soft idleness,
   And on Sunday to call themselves sinners,
And be mothers, ere long, of more fools
To be sent to more " Finishing schools."

Hilda, p. 128.

WINNIE.

SURELY Winnie is changed; we ne'er had been
   friends together,
Had she always been ready to sting like a wasp
   in October weather.
I think there is hardly a name she has not some
   story about—
Of all that we knew long ago—a story suggesting a doubt.
Each face that I used to remember as beaming
   with kindly light,
Is smirched with something or other, and no one
   escapes her spite,
Sneering with scornful laughter, turn wherever
   she may,

All the glory is dimmed of all that come in her
    way;
She creeps on the noblest natures stealthily as
    a cat,
Now with a bite of venom, and now with a
    wanton pat,
Leaving them not till crushed. And one thing I
    cannot abide,
The way that she flatters my husband even when
    I am beside,
Now flopping down on her knees, and staring up
    in his face,
Clasping her hands, and feigning an ecstasy quite
    out of place;
Pumping up tears at his pathos, or sighing with
    heaving breast,
Or giggling and clapping her hands when his
    humour is wickedest.
He is weak enough to believe her, which makes
    me colder in praise,
And I care for poetry less than I ever did all my
    days.
She flatters him daily with words that are silky
    and soft and sleek,
And no true wife can be pleased when seeing her
    husband weak.

'Tis growing quite dreadful to hear her now and
    then, when she speaks
Jauntily of a Faith that needs no God, nor
    seeks
To trace His work on the earth, or follow His
    way on high,

Noting his glorious footprints clear in the starry
    sky ;
For Nature has in herself the reason for all that is,
And God is an unscientific, needless hypothesis,
Like witches, ghosts, and miracles—dreams of the
    slumbrous night
Which the great dawn of reason has driven away
    with its light !

Thereto my husband made answer—and O I was
    proud and glad ;
" Look you, Miss Winnie," he said, "it's your
    method of science that's bad ;
Good for its own end, of course ; but here it is
    clearly at fault ;
God is not found by the tests that detect you an
    acid or salt.
While you search only for secrets that process of
    science sets free,
Nothing you'll find in the world, but matter to
    handle or see.
Here is a book I am reading now ; what can your
    method find there ?
Boil it, or burn it, dissect it, let microscope scan
    it with care ;
What does it show you but paper and ink and
    leather and thread,
All made of chemical simples that, no doubt, you
    have in your head ?
But where is the thought, which is all the end
    and use of the book,
And which flows on through its pages clear to
    my mind as a brook

Rippling and singing sweet music to him that
　　hath ears to hear?
Have you an acid will test it? a glass that will
　　make it all clear?
Or scalpel to cut it?　And yet paper and leather
　　and ink
All are but trash, if I find not the thought which
　　the writer can think.
What, now, if Spirit and God are the thought
　　which is written out plain
On the great page of the world, and your method
　　of seeking is vain?"

Hilda, p. 112.

MISS PENELOPE LEITH.

LAST heiress she of many a rood,
　　Where Ugie winds through Buchan braes—
A treeless land, where beeves are good,
　　And men have quaint old-fashioned ways,
And every burn has ballad-lore,
　　And every hamlet has its song,
And on its surf-beat rocky shore
　　The eerie legend lingers long.
Old customs live there, unaware
　　That they are garments cast away,
And what of light is shining there
　　Is lingering light of yesterday.

Never to her the new day came,
　　Or if it came she would not see;
This world of change was still the same
　　To our old-world Penelope:

New fashions rose, old fashions went,
  But still she wore the same brocade,
With lace of Valenciennes or Ghent
  More dainty by her darning made,
A little patch upon her face,
  A tinge of colour on her cheek,
A frost of powder, just to grace
  The locks that time began to streak.

A stately lady ; to the poor
  Her manner was without reproach ;
But from the Causeway she was sure
  To snub the Provost in his coach :
In pride of birth she did not seek
  Her scorn of upstarts to conceal,
But of a Bailie's wife would speak
  As if she bore the fisher's creel.
She said it kept them in their place,
  Their fathers were of low degree ;
She said the only saving grace
  Of upstarts was humility.

The quaint, old Doric still she used,
  And it came kindly from her tongue ;
And oft the "mim-folk" she abused,
  Who mincing English said or sung :
She took her claret, nothing loth,
  Her snuff that one small nostril curled ;
She might rap out a good round oath,
  But would not mince it for the world :
And yet the wild word sounded less
  In that Scotch tongue of other days ;
Twas just like her old-fashioned dress,
  And part of her old-fashioned ways.

At every fair her face was known,
  Well-skilled in kyloes and in queys ;
And well she led the fiddler on
  To "wale" the best of his strathspeys ;
Lightly she held the man who rose
  While the toast-hammer still could rap,
And brought her gossip to a close,
  Or spoilt her after-dinner nap ;
Tea was for women, wine for men,
  And if they quarrelled o'er their cups,
They might go to the peat-moss then,
  And fight it out like stags or tups.

She loved a bishop or a dean,
  A surplice or a rocket well,
At all the church's feasts was seen,
  And called the Kirk, Conventicle ;
Was civil to the minister,
  But stiff and frigid to his wife,
And looked askance, and sniffed at her,
  As if she lived a dubious life.
But yet his sick her cellars knew,
  Well stored from Portugal or France,
And many a savoury soup and stew
  Her game-bags furnished to the Manse.

But if there was a choicer boon
  Above all else she would have missed,
It was on Sunday afternoon
  To have her quiet game at whist
Close to the window, when the Whigs ·
  Were gravely passing from the Kirk,
And some on foot, and some in gigs,
  Would stare at her unhallowed work :

She gloried in her " devil's books "
　　That cut their sour hearts to the quick :
Rather than miss their wrathful looks
　　She would have almost lost the trick.

Her politics were of the age
　　Of Claverhouse or Bolingbroke ;
Still at the Dutchman she would rage,
　　And still of gallant Grahame she spoke,
She swore 'twas right that Whigs should die
　　Psalm-snivelling in the wind and rain,
Though she would ne'er have harmed a fly
　　For buzzing on the window pane.
And she had many a plaintive rhyme
　　Of noble Charlie and his men :
For her there was no later time,
　　All history had ended then.

The dear old sinner ! yet she had
　　A kindly human heart, I wot,
And many a sorrow she made glad,
　　And many a tender mercy wrought :
And though her way was somewhat odd,
　　Yet in her way she feared the Lord,
And thought she best could worship God
　　By holding Pharisees abhorred,
By being honest, fearless, true,
　　And thorough both in word and deed,
And by despising what is new,
　　And clinging to her old-world creed.

Raban, p. 195.

MIRREN.

SHE was but a maid of all work,
  For she could not bear to see
Idle sluts about her kitchen
  Slopping tables with their tea;
And besides, she had a habit
  Of speaking out her mind
Which might not look respectful
  If another stood behind;
For she'd scold a wasteful mistress
  Very roundly to her face,
But would not let another
  Think a thought to her disgrace.

She had seen her fifty winters,
  But was always trim and tight
In her printed cotton bodice,
  And her apron clean and white:
Never knew her head a bonnet,
  But a cap of muslin thin
With a bit of simple ribbon
  Tied in bows beneath her chin:
And her features, small and puckered,
  Looking tempery and tart,
Did not truly tell the secret
  Of her true and faithful heart.

All the folk that did not know her—
  And there were not many did,
For her faults were somewhat patent,
  And her virtues mainly hid—

Much disliked her prim preciseness,
   And her stiff unchanging ways,
And the tartness of her sayings,
   And the scrimpness of her praise.
But the children whom she rated
   If their boots had soiled her floor,
Knew how fain she was to cheer them,
   When their little hearts were sore.

She had never left the city,
   Rarely seen the growing corn,
Never been a five-miles' journey
   From the spot where she was born,
Never voyaged in a steam-boat,
   Never travelled by the mail,
And nothing could persuade her
   To go jaunting on the rail.
But she knew the streets and closes,
   And the harbour and the boats,
And the kindly fishers' houses,
   And their creels and nets and floats.

And all the grand old mansions
   Where the gentry once would dwell,
With their cork-screw stairs and turrets,
   And their chambers panelled well,
And the stately Lords and Ladies
   Who had ridden from their doors,
And the fateful tragic dramas
   Oft enacted on their floors,
She could tell you stories of them,
   Till a feeling in you woke
That the nobles must have sorrows
   Not allowed to common folk.

Going weekly to the market,
  You might safely trust her care
Not to squander one half penny
  Of your thrifty monies there ;
She would have the best and cheapest,
  Yet she would not chaffer long ;
They might cheat a young housekeeper,
  But they feared her caustic tongue ;
Nor would she for a moment
  Linger in the sun or rain ;
She had gone to do her business,
  And must home to work again.

Going weekly to the kirk too,
  Be the Sunday dry or wet,
With her Bible in her kerchief,
  And her features primly set,
There she sat in tireless patience,
  Thinking less about her sin
Than about her common duties,
  And the frets she had therein,
Not unpleased that she had done them
  With some credit to herself,
And with visions of her saucepans
  All in order on their shelf.

One day she told her mistress,
  She must find another maid :
No, she had no fault to find with
  Any thing they did or said,
And she was not like the fickle
  Fools that wanted just a change,
Nor did she much rebel at
  That new-fangled kitchen range ;

And she had not made her mind up
  To take a place or no;
There was nothing she was sure of,
  Only just that she must go.

Plainly there was something hidden;
  There was mystery in her look;
But she pursed her lips, and held it
  Tight as in a close-sealed book.
They wist not, when she left them,
  What had wiled her thus away,
Puzzling over it, and guessing
  Twenty different things a day;
They were angry, for they missed her,
  Nothing seeming to go smooth;
But the pathos of it touched them,
  When they came to know the truth.

She had served a gentlewoman,
  When they both were fresh and young;
They had smiled and sighed together,
  And together wept and sung.
Proud was Mirren of her mistress
  While her beauty was in bud,
Yet prouder to remember
  She was come of gentle blood,
Having Lords to her forefathers,
  With Ladies by their side,
And loves and wars to tell of,
  And tragic tales to hide.

But the lady, when her beauty
  'Gan to have a faded look,

Mated with a man beneath her,
 Which her handmaid could not brook.
Why could she not live single?
 Maidenhood was clean and sweet;
If wed she must, why pick him
 From the gutter on the street?
She had never served but gentles,
 And she trowed she never would, .
So they quarrelled, and they parted,
 Both of them in angry mood.

So the lady had her wedding,
 Though a stranger dressed her hair,
And a hand she had not proven
 Robed her in her garments fair.
But the marriage-bed was barren,
 And the wedded life was shame,
For he wasted all her substance,
 And he soiled a noble name;
Till friendless and forsaken,
 With a hot and fevered eye,
In weariness and sickness
 She prayed that she might die.

But as she sat despairing
 The door was opened wide,
Then closed again in silence,
 And one stood by her side,
As of old so trim and tidy,
 As of old with bodice bright,
With the dainty cap of muslin,
 And the apron clean and white;

As of old so peppery tempered,
  As of old so prim and tart;
But also underneath it
  Lay the old, true, faithful heart.

And she pushed a bag of something
  Right into the lady's hand,
Saying, "Not a word, Miss Elsie,
  It is by the Lord's command;
I've been toiling, scrimping, saving,
  Till my bones and joints would ache,
And I've put my soul in peril
  All for filthy lucre's sake.
Save me now from that temptation,
  Give my soul a chance of life,
For I've just been self-deceiving,
  Though I have been no man's wife.

"Now get you to the parlour,
  This is not the place for you,
I am mistress of my kitchen,
  And I have my work to do;
Take your seat beside the window;
  There you'll see the breezy bay,
And the brown sails of the fishers
  Dipping in the white sea-spray,
And the children pulling sea-weed,
  And the old men gathering bait,
And lads the old boats mending
  That are in a leaky state,
And the lighthouse on the skerry,
  And the red lamp on the pier,
And the lass that's always waiting
  For the ship that comes not here.
F

" Oh, you'll never weary watching
　　The ships that come and go,
Or to hear the sailors singing
　　As they turn the capstan slow ;
Some are bound for far Archangel,
　　Some for Greenland's snow and ice,
Some, it's likely, for a harbour
　　In the land of Paradise.
But the hand of God is o'er them,
　　And behind them and before,
And the gate of Heaven as near them
　　On the sea as on the shore.

" O my bonnie, sweet Miss Elsie,
　　My blessing and my care,
You'll break my heart now, sitting
　　With that look of hard despair ;
Rouse ye up, there's work to do yet,
　　And peace for you to win,
And the web of life is never
　　Only sorrow warped with sin.
There's sunshine in the rain-cloud,
　　And heat in wreaths of snow,
And God's love is in all things
　　That happen here below."

So Mirren pleaded fondly,
　　And her plea prevailed at last,
And they lived together loving,
　　As they had done in the past.
The lady broidered garments,
　　Or darned the dainty lace,

Which her handmaid washed as no one
  Could wash in all the place;
And if their fare was scanty,
  No eye was there to see,
As they held themselves aloof still
  In pride of poverty.

Trim was still the lady's raiment,
  Never seeming to grow worse,
And she never lacked the glitter
  Of a gold-piece in her purse;
And on the Bishop's visit
  She could give him rare old tea—
For of course she went to Chapel
  Duly with the Quality.
The Bishop for her lady
  Was the fitting minister;
But the Kirk was still to Mirren
  The house of God for her.

So the weeks went by in patience,
  And the Sabbaths brought their peace,
And the years sped lightly o'er them,
  Though their labours did not cease;
And in the summer mornings
  They saw the sun rise red,
And the sea a golden pavement,
  Whereon his feet might tread;
And in the winter evenings
  O'er their needles and their frames
They told most tragic stories
  Of the old-world knights and dames.

And their way of life was tranquil,
   And their thoughts were pure and sweet,
And the poor that lived beside them
   Thought the better of the street,
When the gentry came to see them,
   And the great world, in the pride
Of its carriages and horses,
   Drew the children to its side ;
Though a grander world was inside
   If they had but eyes to see
The faith and love that dwelt there,
   And true-hearted piety.

Heretic, p. 173.

DESCRIPTIVE PIECES.

ABERDEEN.

THERE'S an old University town
  Between the Don and the Dee
Looking over the grey sand dunes,
  Looking out on the cold North Sea.
  Breezy and blue the waters be,
And rarely there you shall not find
The white horse-tails lashing out in the wind,
Or the mists from the land of ice and snow
Creeping over them chill and slow.
Sitting o' nights in his silent room,
The student hears the lonesome boom
Of breaking waves on the long sand reach,
And the chirming of pebbles along the beach ;
And gazing out on the level ground,
Or the hush of keen stars wheeling round,
He *feels* the silence in the sound.

So, hearkening to the City's stir,
Alone in some still house of God
Whose solemn aisles are only trod
By rarely-coming worshipper,

At times, beneath the fret and strife,
The far-off hum, the creaking wain,
The hurrying tread of eager gain,
And all the tide of alien life,
We catch the Eternal Silence best,
And unrest only speaks of rest.

O'er the College Chapel a grey stone crown
Lightsomely soars above tree and town,
Lightsomely fronts the Minster towers,
Lightsomely chimes out the passing hours
To the solemn knell of their deep-toned bell;
Kirk and College keeping time,
Faith and Learning, chime for chime.
The Minster stands among the graves,
And its shadow falls on the silent river;
The Chapel is girt with Life's bounding waves,
And the pulses of hope there are passioning
    ever.—
But death is life, and life is death;
Being is more than a gasp of breath:
We come and go, we are seen and lost,
Now in glimmer, and now in gloom;
But oft this body is the tomb,
And the Life is with the silent host.
So to living and dead let the solemn bell call;
Sleeping or waking, time passes with all.

Borland Hall, p. 3.

THE CATHEDRAL TOWN.

A GREY old Minster on the height
Towers o'er the trees and in the light;
A grey old town along the ridge
Slopes, winding downward to the bridge—
    A quaint, old, gabled place.
    With Church stamped on its face.

The quiet Close, secluded, dim,
The lettered scroll, the pillar slim,
The armorial bearings on the wall,
The very air you breathe, are all
    Full of Church memories,
    And the old sanctities.

And beautiful the grey old place
With characters of antique grace,
That tell the tale of pious work
Beneath the spire and round the kirk,
    And growth of Law and Right
    Where Christ had come with light.

Begrimed with smoke, a monotone
Of equal streets in brick or stone,
With squalid lane, and flaunting Hall,
Infrequent spire, and chimneys tall;
    You know the place wherein
    The weary toil and spin.

With jalousie and portico,
And oriel large, where sea-winds blow,
And light parade, and ample streets,
Where idler with the idler meets ;
    You know the haunt of pleasure,
    Or sick resort of leisure.

Far otherwise the old church town,
With the grey minster for its crown :
Its tide of work has ebbed away ;
Its pleasuring was never gay ;
    Yet there the morning broke,
    And the new world awoke.

And it is well, amid the whirr
Of restless wheels and busy stir,
To find a quiet spot where live
Fond pious thoughts conservative,
    That ring to an old chime,
    And bear the moss of time.

Like ivy clasping ruin grey,
And greenly clothing its decay ;
Like garden haunted to this hour
With smell of some old-fashioned flower ;
    So sweet the dim old town
    Still with its minster crown.

There is a strange philosophy
Among the wondrous things that be ;
Even that the path which man has trod
Progresses still away from God,
    And that we flourish most
    As piety is lost.

As sacred turns to secular,
As worship wanes, and temples are
Unvisited and voiceless grown,
And only rigid law is known :
    Even so, they say, do we
    Achieve our destiny.

Alas ! and must the deep divine
Impress of God, and the grand line
Of our high parentage be lost,
To reach the meagre winning-post
    Of modern social saw,
    And economic law?

Nay, but in this quaint place I see
The nobler thought of history ;
The birth of civil right and peace,
And progress that shall never cease,
    Amid the chaunt and hymn
    In cloistered alley dim.

And sweeter far and grander too
The ancient civilization grew,
With holy war and busy work
Beneath the spire and round the kirk,
    Than miles of brick and stone
    In godless monotone.

For here, in wild and lawless days,
The Culdee waked a psalm of praise
For Gospel light and liberty,
And help of man's great misery ;
    And Darkness from its throne
    Fled at the Cross alone.

So was it then—so is it now,
And will for ever be, I trow:
The only spell of might is He,
The watchword and the victory;
        And thou shalt suffer loss,
        But conquer in the Cross.

Back rolls the Darkness, as they come,
The victor griefs of Christendom;
Omnipotent sorrows only heal
The evils of the common weal;
        And dim and ever dimmer
        All other lights shall glimmer.

The good monk had his working day,
The good priest also passed away,
The mitre faded, and the crook,
And chanted hymn, and lettered book;
        But in this quiet place
        They left a natural grace.

A quaint old place—a minster grey,
And grey old town that winds away,
Through gardens, down the sloping ridge
To river's brim and ancient bridge,
        Where the still waters flow
        To the deep pool below.

                        The Bishop's Walk, p. 1.

IONA.

LONE, green Isle of the West,
  Where the Monks, their corracle steering,
Could see no more, o'er the wave's white crest,
  Their own loved home in Erin ;
Shrouded often in mist,
  And buried in cloud and rain ;
Yet once by the light of a glory kissed,
  Which nothing can dim again !

O'er tangled and shell-paved rocks
  The white sea-gulls are flying ;
And in the sunny coves brown flocks
  Of wistful seals are lying ;
The waves are breaking low,
  Hardly their foam you trace ;
All hushed and still, as if they know
  This is a sacred place.

The diving guillemot
  Is preening his dappled feather ;
The great merganser shows his throat,
  Red in this summer weather ;
And bathed in a tremulous light
  Are minster, cross, and grave,
That call up the past with a spell of might,
  To tell of the meek and brave.

No fitter day than this
  To look on thy mystic beauty,
And brood on memories of the bliss
  Of faith and love and duty,

Of the hours of quiet prayer,
  Of the days of patient toil,
Of the love that always, and everywhere,
  Burned like a holy oil.

O lone green Isle of the West,
  So oft by the mist enshrouded,
I have seen thee to-day in thy quiet best,
  Not noisily mobbed, and crowded,
Seen thee in flooding light,
  Seen thee in perfect calm ;
Yet am I sad as at the sight
  Of mummy that men embalm.

Isle of the past and gone,
  The life from thee has departed ;
Thy best is now but a carven stone,—
  And a memory lonely-hearted !
Yet thou wert a power erewhile,
  O'er the great world's mind and heart ;
But where now the priests of the Holy Isle
  And the skill of its graceful Art ?

Skilled was the hand that wrought
  Your traceried tombs and crosses,
And silvern brooches that yet are brought
  From depths of the black peat mosses ;
And theirs was a holy work
  Who carried the gospel pure   ·
Where the white waves break by the old White-
    kirk,
  And brought salvation sure.

Was it the Norseman's sword,
  And the ships of Thor and Odin
That drove the saints with the sacred Word
  From the peaceful ways they trod in?
Was it the Saxon's sway,
  Brutal and selfish and strong,
That swept the beautiful Art away,
  And stifled the Celtic song?

Only this do we know,
  The Celt brought light to the Teuton,
And ever the knowledge of God did grow
  In the land he set his foot on;
But as they throve he pined,
  But as they smiled he sighed,
But as they grew he surely dwined,
  And in their life he died.

O passion of holy love!
  O sacrificial people,
Dying to lift men's thoughts above
  By altar and cross and steeple!
Through stormy seas ye passed,
  And moor and marsh and fen,
To be left behind in the march at last
  As weak exhausted men!

They say ye shall rise again
  On the level Western prairie,
With a larger life and a keener brain,
  Like eagle out of his eyrie;

But not the mind and the heart
   That grew by the Lochs and Bens,
Nor the plaintive song and the mystic Art
   Nursed in the rushy glens.

North Country Folk, p. 239.

HILDA'S HOME.

OUR home is a bright little cottage, half-smothered
   in yellow rose,
Not yet blooming, however; a still river sullenly
   flows
Deep at the foot of a broomy brae, and the
   leaping trout
Ripple its gloom in the evening as May-flies
   flicker about.
Nor is it all so sullen, for down in a farther
   reach
It leaps and sparkles and gleams o'er the stones
   of a pebbly beach,
Under the birch and the hazel, just coming to
   leaf, and there are
Blue-bell patches of sky made bright with the
   primrose star.
Behind is a group of great fir-trees, five of them,
   red-armed firs,—
Druid sisters he calls them,—that moan when
   the night-wind stirs ;
Last of a great pine forest that stubs the heath
   with its roots
For miles, till you come to a tarn where gulls
   and little round coots

Are dipping and diving all day in a quiet
    solitude ;
There the bee haunts, and the air is blithe, and
    the lapwings brood.
I hear the curlew scream, and the grouse-cock
    crowing at dawn,
And yet when I stand at the door, where the
    cowslips laugh on the lawn—
It is only a patch of green turf, enough to
    pasture a lark—
I see the sleepy old town, and the spires of the
    Minster dark,
And catch a glimpse of the sea-waves white on
    the yellow sand,
Where the river leaps at the bar, and the coast-
    guard houses stand.
We have a bright little garden down on a sunny
    slope,
Bordered with sea-pinks, and sweet with the
    songs and the blossoms of hope.
O it is all too good for me; often I catch myself
    singing
In very lightness of heart, and I seem like the
    birds to be winging
Merry from room to room, as they flutter from
    bush to tree,
And each has her mate a-coming, and mine, too,
    is coming to me.

Am I wrong to be always so happy? This
    world is full of grief;
Yet there is laughter of sunshine, to see the
    crisp green on the leaf,

Daylight is ringing with song-birds, and brooklets
    are crooning by night;
And why should I make a shadow where God
    makes all so bright?
Earth may be wicked and weary, yet I cannot
    help being glad;
There is sunshine without and within me, and
    how should I mope or be sad?
God would not flood me with blessings, meaning
    me only to pine
Amid all the bounties and beauties He pours
    upon me and mine;
Therefore will I be grateful, and therefore will I
    rejoice;
My heart is singing within me; sing on, O heart
    and voice.

Hilda, p. 60.

EVENING WALKS.

WE have walks as the evenings lengthen; some-
    times over the moor,
Many-tinted and shadowed; brisk is the air there
    and pure
Among the brown heath and the bracken that
    now from its snake-like bonds,
Under the sun's deft fingers, is slowly uncoiling
    its fronds;
Close-packed now, by-and-by they, overlapping,
    will hide
The flower of the slender orchis purpling close
    by their side.

Dry on the knolls is the whin-bush, massing its
    golden bloom ;   .
The cotton-grass low in the marshes tosses its
    small white plume ;
And from the hollows is wafted the scent of bog-
    myrtle or birch
Fragrant after the rain ; but, best of all, is the
    search
Among the roots of the heather for stag-moss
    antlers green
Branching over the earth, far-spreading, and rarely
    seen.
Here and there is a cottage, too, looking just
    like the heath,
Green on the roof with house-leek, brown with
    its turf-wall beneath.
Children play at the door, they are dirty and
    happy and fair,
Sunbrowned all of their faces, sunbleached their
    lint-white hair ;
The mother is milking the cow, the dog lies
    coiled in the sun,
The fowls for the roost are making, and the
    labourer's day is done.
Sometimes we rest on a bank, and hear in the
    evening calm,
Just as the stars come out, the *sough* of their
    grateful psalm.

Often we go to the sea-marge, where the long
    sands give place
To a belt of dark red crags, storm-beaten, which
    grimly face

G

The baffled billows that lie ever panting below
    at their feet,
Or gurgling in black-throated caves where they
    foam and mine and beat.
Perched on the cliff is a village, and far in the
    cove below
The boats are beached on the shingle, waiting
    the tide to flow ;
Hard-visaged, bunchy women are baiting the
    lines in hope,
Or carrying laden creels, slow, up the long, shelv-
    ing slope,
Or spreading their fish on the rocks, or wel-
    coming men from the sea,
As the lugger trips daintily in, and the flapping
    sail is free.

One thing strikes me about my husband's way
    with the folk,
Whether the moorland shepherds, or fishermen
    perched on the rock.
Freely we enter their homes, for he seems to be
    known to them all,
And knows who is there in the corner, and who
    in the bed in the wall,
And the idiot dreamily singing by the grandam
    racked with pain,
And the lad that went off to the sea, and has
    never come back again—
All the home life of the people, their good and
    their evil hap.
So every door flies open just after a warning
    tap,

And everywhere he is met with a welcome glad
 and free ;
The dogs come fawning upon him, the children
 get up on his knee,
Great, rough hands are held out to give him a
 hearty grip,
And the mother's face is shining as he kisses the
 baby's lip.
Of course they are happy to see me, too, for my
 husband's sake,
Only they daintily touch me, as fearful perchance
 I may break,
And, making ungainly curtseys, they have not a
 word to say ;
But O I am proud to see him so loved in this
 lovingest way.

        Hilda, p. 65.

THE STORM.

FROM every part of heaven the clouds crept,
 slow, across the sky,
  Black clouds, with lurid edges, and rifts of
  leaden grey,
And earth lay still and breathless as they mus-
 tered there on high,
  Nor lark nor throstle noting the dimly dying
  day.

Then all was wrapt in darkness, without twinkling
 of a star,

And the big thunder-rain came down in sullen
    warning drops ;
Beneath the silent trees the silent kine were
    grouped, and far
    The sea moaned, and a shiver passed along
    the tall tree-tops.

And then it burst in fury—rain and hailstones
    mixed with fire,
    And sudden gusts of wind that howled across
    the stony moor,
With awful lulls, and shattering peals that nearer
    grew and higher ;
    And one great ball of hissing fire fell almost
    at the door.

A wild, black night of tempest, such as men
    remember long
    In the dull undated life of a sleepy country
    town,
When forests fell before the wind, streams swept
    off bridges strong,
    And church-towers, lightning-shivered, reeled,
    and then came crashing down.

Awe-stricken, yet entranced, I watched, with
    tremulous joy, each phase
    And movement as it registered itself upon the
    mind,
While the strained sense, exulting in the wonder
    and amaze,
    Jarred at a common sound amid the thunder
    and the wind.

Hilda, p. 183.

A HIGHLAND FUNERAL.

POOR fishers on the wild west shore
  Where slow mists trail along the hills,
And from the mist comes evermore
  The sound of rushing brooks and rills,
Are plodding, grave, with lingering feet,
  About the high hot noon of day,
Along the circle of the street
  That straggles round the circling bay.

Why are the long-oared boats afloat?
  Why tolls the bell from the steepled kirk?
It is not the hour to launch the boat,
  And it is not the Sabbath of rest from work ;
And why are they all in best array,
As it were for some high holiday?
'Neath crags and hills the long loch winds,
  Through rocky isles where sea-birds flock ;
Along the slopes the grey birch finds
  Frail footing on the slaty rock ;
On every ledge there grows a pine,
  With roots that cling as the branches toss,
And the oaks along the low sea-line
  Are greenly feathered with fern and moss.
Behind the cliffs are mountains steep
  By foaming torrents scored and scarred,
And up their gullies the alders creep,
  But the peaks are ragged and jagged and
    barred :
Cloud-capped often their stormy tops,
  While ridge and corrie and crag are bare,
Or a girdle of mist will ring the slopes,
  While the heights rise clear in the upper air.

A desolate land of fern and moss,
  Of brackened braes and craggy hills,
And shores where fickle waters toss,
  And birch-and-hazel-fringéd rills
And foaming cataracts like snow
  That in the gorges leap and run,
And rocks, ice-polished long ago,
  That gleam like waters in the sun,
And rainbows arching high in heaven
  And down in still lochs doubly bowed,
While broken prismic lights are woven
  On the thin veils of wavering cloud,
And gorgeous sunsets that enfold
  The mountains with a purple robe,
And dash the crimson and the gold
  In billowy spray about the globe:
A land of wayside cairns—the place
  Of resting for the biers of death—
And tokens of a fading race,
  And relics of forgotten faith—
Legend and rhyme and mystic rite,
  The worship of a God unknown,
Stealthily done at dead of night
  By sacred well or standing stone.
O marvel not they love the land
  Who watch its changeful hills and skies,
For in its desolation grand
  A charm of 'wildering beauty lies.

A meagre life they have, and still— ·
  Not stiller almost is the grave—
Those villagers beneath the hill
  That looks down on the encircling wave;

Rude are the huts of stone and turf
  That straggle round the circling street.
The thatched roofs soaked with rain or surf,
  And blackened with the smoking peat.
No ploughshare tears the scanty soil,
  Enough for them are spade and hoe;
'Tis on the waters that they toil,
  And in the seas their harvests grow.
The moors are for the hare and grouse,
  The corries for the antlered stag,
But shaggy big-horned cattle browse
  On the fringe of bracken and rush and flag.
And now and then comes like a dream
  A white-sailed yacht into the bay,
And now and then the snort of steam
  Sounds from the headland far away;
But never shows the world's proud strife,
  Its strain of power and rush of thought:
Time counts for nothing in their life,
  But comes and goes, and changes nought.
Yet men have grown there, true and brave,
  Bronzed with weather, and horny of hand,
Who wrestled with the problems grave
  That at the porch of Wisdom stand;
And you shall find in low, thatched cot,
  Round-angled, and with smoke begrimed,
Love that can sweeten every lot,
  And Faith that hath all fates sublimed.

But why are the long-oared boats afloat?
  Why tolls the bell from the steepled kirk?
It is not the hour to launch the boat,
  And it is not the Sabbath of rest from work;

And why are the children sad and grave,
With no ripple of mirth by the rippling wave?
And whither away do the strong men walk,
While the women gather in groups and talk?

.   .   .   .

Slowly the muffled oars dip in the tide,
Slowly the silent boats shadow-like glide
Past the grey, steepled kirk, past the low manse,
Now in the ripples that glimmer and glance
Where the sun flashes, and now in the shade
The birch-feathered rocks and the great hills
        have made;
Slowly and silently onward they pass
Over the calm spaces shining like glass,
While wild wailing strains of the coronach swell,
And fall with the breeze and the slow-tolling bell.
Long, low and dark is the first of the train,
With six bending oars keeping time to the strain;
In it a coffin, and by it a maiden
Who to the moaning sea moans sorrow-laden,
As they drop down to the dim abbey pile
Lying half-hid in a cleft of the isle,
Ruined and roofless, 'mid tangle of trees
That dip their low boughs in the wave, but the
        breeze
Rustles their higher leaves over a tower
Green with massed ivy, and crown'd with wall-
        flower.
There, with his forefathers, peaceful to sleep
By the white surf of the unresting deep,
Where once the Culdee monk toiled, prayed, and
        died,
Where once the galleys oared out in their pride,

Where still the clansmen their high chiefs bewail,
Silent they laid the good priest of the Gael.
No cross was reared above his head,
No requiem was sung or said,
No hope was spoken of the just
In glory rising from the dust :
In silent awe they did their part,
Yet the good hope was in every heart.

Kildrostan, pp. 1 and 10.

FAILURE.

I SEE the Kirk beneath the hill,
   The tall elms rustling in the breeze,
The modest Manse, so calm and still,
The dripping of the sleepy mill
   That hides among the nutting trees.

I look down, with a hungry heart,
   On the broad river rippling cool ;
The fisher plies his patient art,
The trout leaps, and the May flies dart
   About the slowly eddying pool.

Low sunbeams on the meadows play,
   The moon shows like a film of cloud,
A star from the red skirts of day
Peeps to another star far away,
   And the hill is wrapt in a misty shroud.

A shepherd's wife comes to the door,
   Shading her eyes with large brown hand,

He is away on the upland moor,
And nothing she sees but a kestrel soar,
  Keen-eyed, spying over the land.

There is no voice but the rushing rills,
  And creak of frightened peewit's wing,
And bleat of young lambs on the hills,
Heard only when a silence fills
  The soul, and all the space of things,

What made my eyes grow dim and blind?—
  Ah, when the heart is heavy and low,
The beauty that on earth we find,
Or strain of music on the wind,
  Shall touch it like an utter woe!

                              Kaban, p. 61.

A WALK.

A CLEAR, crisp, Autumn day. Autumn is Scotch
And lingers lovingly among the hills,
Knee-deep in golden bracken, and golden grass
That tints the moor, what time the purple heather
Withers to brown, and golden pendants hang
On the slim, drooping birch—the golden time
Of all the Northern year.

              You shall find Spring,
Joyous with bursting life, in English lanes.
Where the May-blossom wafts from straggling
        hedge
Its incense like a white-robed Thurifer,

While the meek violet, like a saintly soul,
Hid in a green obscurity, breathes out
Its sweets, unseen, and the pale primrose woos
The shadow at the foot of lush blue-bells.
Green are the meadows there, and green the leaves
Opening, with various shade, in chestnut whorles,
And feathery birch, aud plane and beech and lime,
And late ash-bud and oak—the many tints
Like many colours, yet one flush of green
From the young life o' the year.

But Autumn loves
The ferny braes, the brown heath on the hills,
The lichened rocks, orange and grey and black,
The harebell and the foxglove in the shaws,
The brisk and nimble air upon the moor,
The flying cloud that scuds across the blue,
Its shadow hurrying o'er the sunlight brow
Of the still mountain, and the sleepy loch
Quivering as in a dream of coot and tern,
Or leaping trout ; thither the antlered stag
Leads forth his hinds to water at the dawn :
And life is at full pitch of beauty then,
When verging to its close.

That Autumn day,
I wandered forth alone, in sober ways
While yet the shadow of the houses fell
Around me, and the window-eyes looked on ;
Yet I was glad, for I had found my work.
And when I reached the country, and beheld
The loaded wains with the last harvest-sheaves
Led homeward, and the reapers blithe and brown,
And felt my feet among the rustling leaves

By the wayside, and watched the shining spikes
Of frost in shady nooks beside the burn,
I could not walk, but leaped, and laughed at
    nothings
In very joy of life; for anything
Serves for a jest what time the heart is gay.

So on and up I went, with tireless feet,
And fertile mind suggesting victories
My pen should win for me, as the slow years
Ripened the powers which circumstance disclosed,
And critics now approved. I had the trick
Of hoping to the full, and building up
Dream-palaces, creative, out of nothing,
Collapsing into nothing at a touch
Of adverse fact; and that day I was in
The mood to make whole worlds, with suns and
    stars,
And flowers and birds, and homes by love made
    glad.

But crossing a waste moor, where hills of slag
Rose bare, and sluggish pools were at their feet,
Where no fish swam, but red lights ever glowed,
I came upon a village mean and poor,
Which no one cared for, save to draw much wealth
From seams of coal, and veins of ironstone
That undermined it; one long string of huts,
Ugly and dirty and monotonous;
And no bell rang there on the Sabbath morn,
And only Death e'er spoke to them of God.
Swart, stunted men were plodding from the pits,
Weary, with little lamps stuck in their caps
Instead of flower or feather; savage children

Were skulking at the doors, but none of them
Did run to meet their fathers, and be kissed
And borne home shoulder-high ; the mothers, too,
Were fierce, and smiled not when the men came
    home,
For they were weary, and not with woman's work.
Oft had I seen the peasant from his plough
Plod slowly home, but gladdened by his girl,
Curly and sunny, chattering at his side,
And by the baby nestling on his breast,
And by the mother smiling at the door
With the milk-pail ; and often watched the fisher,
Hard-faced and weather-beaten, leave his boat,
At early morn with children gambolling,
Bare-footed, on the sand, or leading him
Home in the pride of love, with the fresh spoils
Of the old sea ; but such a sight as this,
So without hope or heart or any joy
I had not seen before : a place so dreary,
So God-forsaken in its ugliness,
Each house alike, the people too alike
Dismal and brutal ; and the only spot
With any brightness was a drinking house
Shining with glass and brass and painted barrels.

Therewith the thought again knocked at my heart,
Urgent and loud : Was thy life given to thee
For making pretty sentences, and play
Of dainty humour for the mirthful heart
To be more merry ; or to serve thy kind,
Redressing wrong ? And all the long way home
That thought kept ever knocking at my heart.

Raban, p. 125.

DRAMATIC FRAGMENTS.

LOQUITUR THOROLD.

'TWAS sweet to dream as we have dreamed
　Together in years long ago,
When life might be, as Fancy deemed,
　For aught the happy child could know,
　A bright illusion, and a show
Create at will, and shaped to meet
Each changeful whim, and quaint conceit,
　And varying mood of joy or woe,
Nor ever with tragic end complete.

But ill for him who will not see
　The dream to be a dream indeed,
And life a fateful mystery,
　And iron fact the only creed
　To lean on in the hour of need.
The child may dream ; the man must act
With reverence for the world's great fact ;
　And look to toil and sweat and bleed,
And gather his energies all compact.

Olrig Grange, p. 14.

O HAPPY childhood ! wakening first
  In moony realms of fond romance ;
And quenching soon a deeper thirst
  In science that refrained to glance
  Scorn at old faiths : so we could once
Believe we heard the mermaid sing,
And that the deft Fays shaped the ring
  Footing o' moonlights in the dance,
And that Spirit lay hidden in every thing.

Nor need that early faith be all
  In definite, clear knowledge lost :
Though never Greek to Ilium's wall
  In the swift ships the sea had crossed,
  Each wrathful king with banded host,
The tale of Troy were true to me,
More than bare fact of history :
  There is more truth than is engrossed
In your musty sheepskin guarantee.

And there is truth transcending far
  The way of scientific thought,
Which travels to the farthest star,
  And verges on the smallest mote,
  But all beyond it knoweth not ;
Its ladder, based on earth, must lean
Its summit on the felt and seen ;
  But ever our hearts their rest have sought
In that dim Beyond, where it hath not been.

'Tis wisdom, doubtless, for the man
  To learn the fact and steadfast Law ;
Yet Wisdom also in its plan
  Embraced the child's great wondering awe
  Which found the Unseen in all it saw,

Whom now we seek with cruel strain
Of longing heart and wildered brain,
  Tossing our barren chaff and straw
In search of the old diviner grain.

  Can it be wisdom to forget
    What wisdom taught us yesterday?
What if the form may change, and yet
    The truth abide that in it lay?
    And what if Gin, and Ghost, and Fay,
Were but the form of highest truth—
The Father's parable for youth,
    To teach that Law is Will, to say,
I am the worker of all, in sooth!

  So might the dream be, after all,
    The key which confident Science lost,
And hath been groping round the wall
    Of mystery, perplex'd and toss'd,
    In search of, making many a boast,
Yet conscious that her universe
Of several facts and laws is scarce
    God's living world; yea, is at most
His graveyard, whither she drove His hearse.

  Our Science knows no Father yet;
    He seems to vanish as we think;
And most of all, when we are set
    To fish for Faith upon the brink
    Of Nature; we draw, link by link,
A line of close-plied reasoning
Elaborate, and hope to bring,
    Besides the baited thought we sink,
God from the depths at the end of a string!

Ah! who shall find the perfect Whole
  In the small fragment that we see?
Or mirror in the flesh-bound soul
  The image of Immensity?
  Our hearts within us faint, and we,
Amid the storm and darkness driven,
Cry out for God to earth and heaven;
  But what if all our answer be
Only our cry by the echoes given?

As light outside the Temple vast
  Coming and going, with sudden gleams
On altar, pillar, and pavement cast,
  Down on our lower world He streams
  An externe glory. So it seems;
But who can tell? The things that press
On our dream-life's half-consciousness,
  Though real as the hills and streams,
Are the stuff dreams are made of nevertheless.

               Olrig Grange, p. 23.

BUT my Faith is not gone, although
  At times it seems to fade away.
I would I were as long ago;
  I cling to God, and strive to say
  The devil and all his reasons Nay:
But in the crucible of thought
Old forms dissolve, nor have I got,
  Or seem to wish, new moulds of clay
To limit the boundless truth I sought.

Can the great God be aught but vague,
  Bounded by no horizon, save
          H

What feeble minds create to plague
   High Reason with? We madly crave
   For definite truth, and make a grave, .
Through too much certainty precise,
And logical distinction nice,
   For all the little Faith we have,
Buying clear views at a terrible price.

   Too dear, indeed, to part with Faith
      For forms of logic about God,
And walk in lucid realms of death,
      Whose paths incredible are trod
      By no soul living. Faith's abode
Is mystery for evermore,
Its life to worship and adore,
      And meekly bow beneath the rod,
When the day is dark, and the burden sore.

   What soft, low notes float everywhere
      In the soft glories of the moon !
Soft winds are whispering in the air,
      And murmuring waters softly croon
      To mossy banks a muffled tune ;
Softly a rustling faint is borne
Over the fields of waving corn—
      God's still small voice, we drown at noon,
Which is everywhere heard in the even and morn.

   Hush ! let us go. The stars shine out, .
      Yonder the moonlight on the sea,— ·.
The fishers spread their sails about
      Its tangled rings ; from yon lime tree
      The hum of some belated bee

Sways as if lost ; I seem to hear
A boding murmur in my ear
　　Of coming storm. What, if it be
Omen of tempest in my career?

　　Strange ! that whene'er the hour arrives,
　　　Which we have longed for day and night,
　　To act the purpose of our lives,
　　　Fades all the glory and the light,
　　　Fails too the sense of power and might ;
　　And there are omens in the air,
　　And voices whispering Beware !—
　　　But never victor in the fight
Heeded the portents of fear and care.

Olrig Grange, p. 31.

　　MY sun sinks without clouds or fears ;
　　　No spectral shadows gather round
　　The gateway of the endless years,
　　　Where we, long blindfold, are unbound,
　　　And lay our swathings on the ground,
　　To face the Eternal. So I rest
　　Peacefully on the Strong One's breast,
　　　Even though the mystery profound
Ever a mystery be confessed.

　　My old doubts?—Well, they no more fret,
　　　Nor chafe and foam o'er sunken rocks.
　　I don't know that my Faith is yet
　　　Quite regular and orthodox ;
　　　I have not keys for all the locks,
　　And may not pick them. Truth will bear
　　Neither rude handling, nor unfair

Evasion of its wards, and mocks
Whoever would falsely enter there.

But all through life I see a Cross,
  Where sons of God yield up their breath :
Their is no gain except by loss,
  There is no life except by death,
  There is no vision but by Faith,
Nor glory but by bearing shame,
Nor justice but by taking blame ;
  And that Eternal Passion saith,
" Be emptied of glory and right and name."

Olrig Grange, p. 201.

I WONDER how the twilight shines
  On the tinkling brook that cleaves the hill,
And how it rays with great broad lines
  Through rifted clouds that slumber still,
  And how the fall that turned our mill
Glistens, and how the shadows fold
Around the dew as night grows cold,
  And how the lark with tuneful bill
Sings o'er the meadows we loved of old.

I ever loved our earth, and still
  I love its scaurs and brooks and braes,
The long bleak moor, the misty hill,
  And all their creatures, and their ways,
  And many waters sounding praise ;
It seems as if my lingering feet
Clung to its moss and grasses sweet,
  And ferny glades, and golden days
When cowslips and ladybirds made our hearts
  beat.

Throw up the window ; let me hear
  The mellow ouzel once more sing,
The carol of the sky-lark clear,
  The hum of insects on the wing,
  The lowing of the kine to bring
The milk-maid singing with her pail,
The tricksy lapwing's far-off wail,
  The woodland cushat's murmuring,
And the *whish* of the pines in the evening gale.

Fain would I carry with me all
  Blithe Nature's blended harmony ;
The half-notes and the tremulous fall
  Of her young voices, and the free
  Gush of full-throated melody ;
And like a child, I'm loath to go,
And leave the elders to the flow
  Of speech and song and memory,
And take me to sleep in the room below.

Olrig Grange, p. 203.

LOQUITUR MATER DOMINA.

But women who have lost their Faith
  Are angels who have lost their wings,
And always have a nasty breath
  Of chemistry, and horrid things
  That go off when a lecturer rings
His bell.—But *they* will not go off ;
They take a mission or a cough ;
  For men will marry a fool that sings,
Sooner than one that has learnt to scoff.

You don't believe me : you go in
  For science, culture, common-sense,
And think a woman sure to win
  Because she knows the why and whence,
  And looks at vermin through a lens :
And yet you've seen a score of girls
With empty heads, and silly curls,
  And laughter light, and judgment dense,
Wedded to Marquises, Dukes, and Earls.

And why? They started fair with you :—
  You dressed as well—for that was mine ;
You were as handsome and well-born, too,
  And you had wit like sparkling wine :
  But they all took to things divine
Like sober, pious girls. I know
That some were High Church, and would go,
  Like nuns, with beads and crosses fine—
But they all were wives in a season or so.

Men may be bad, but still they like
  A pious wife that lives for heaven ;
Your wit may shine, your beauty strike,
  But not to these their love is given.
  Ah ! had you with your prayer-book driven
To church, and kept a Sunday-school,
And visited, and lived by rule—
  But that is past and all forgiven,
Though you played your cards like a perfect fool.

You cannot be a hypocrite,
  To mumble out a false remorse,
And wear a look of prim conceit
  Only to be the winning horse?—
  Of course, you cannot, and of course

I never meant you should. But yet,
  You might feel true grief and regret
    For sin ; and could be none the worse
For the strawberry leaves in a coronet.

Olrig Grange, p. 81.

NAY, tell me not you do not care
  Although the end of the world were come.
It's very wicked to despair ;
    You should be gentle, patient, dumb,
    Thinking that any day the hum
Of angels, and of saintly crowds,
With rainbow trimmings round their shrouds,
    May greet you at a kettle-drum,
Coming in glory among the clouds.

Olrig Grange, p. 87.

LOQUITUR ROSE.

I HATE a sham ; let bad be bad,
  And good be good for evermore :
Who doeth right, let him be glad,
    Knowing the good he liveth for ;
    Who doeth wrong, let him, too, pour
Unshrinking light upon his ill,
And do it with determined will :—
    But our devil clings to his ways of yore,
And is fain to appear the good angel still.

Olrig Grange, p. 141.

YET mine is not a love like thine,
　　Which brooks no rival, fears no ill,
Which time would mellow like old wine,
　　Which hath no separate end or will,
　　And is content with loving still.
Such life would grow insipid soon
To me, and tiresome as a tune
　　Ground on a barrel-organ, till
A change were as welcome as flowers in June.

It should not, but I know it would ;
　　It seems as if some evil spell
Were on me, holding me from good,
　　And from the peace unspeakable ;
　　There is that in me like a bell
Cracked in the belfry, where it swings
Shaming its office, for it rings,
　　For Christmas cheer and passing knell,
The same false note for all truest things.

Women are fickle—I am more ;
　　Women are contrary—I am worse ;
Even ficklest women can adore,
　　And in adoring gain a force
　　Which holds them to a steadfast course ;
But I've no reverence ; mine eyes
Have only learnt to criticise,
　　To find out flaws, and trace their source,
And to weary of folk that are good and wise.

I love enough to part with pain,
　　But not enough to wed thee poor ;
I dare not face the way of men
　　Who nobly labour and endure,
　　Seeking the great life high and pure.

But I have one true purpose yet ;
I will nòt lead you to forget
    The splendid hope of glory sure,
Which was all your thought until we two met.

Ah ! you will not believe the truth,
    Because it shows me poor and mean ;
You've dreamt that I am all in sooth,
    Which I have dreamt I might have been ;
    And should, perhaps, if I had seen
In early years the generous life
Of aspiration high, and strife
    For truth and love and faith serene,
Which oft you have pictured for you and your wife.
                        Olrig Grange, p. 150.

I COULD not bear the poky rooms
    Where Bloomsbury students talk and smoke,
I'd sicken at the steamy fumes,
    The maid-of-all-work would evoke ;
    I'd sooner hear a raven croak
Than hearken to the flow of wit,
And watch the gleams of genius flit,
    While shabby artist fellows broke
The silence with laughter loud and fit.

'Twas nice, of course, to hear from you
    About their wild Bohemian ways ;
One likes to know how people do
    Who are not in our world. We gaze
    Upon their splendid works, and praise
Their genius, and we long to hear
About their naughty vices dear,

So charming in our books and plays,
Like beings quite in another sphere.

You do not like this tone? I know
    You hate a false, affected vein ;
What, then, if we were bound to row,
    Like galley-slaves, together, twain
    Linked each to each by loathsome chain ;
And by that union sundered more,
Until the fretting bondage wore
    Your heart, and left an aching pain,
As the only trace of the love you bore?

It may not be, it may not be ;
    'Twere grievous sin in me to wed
A soul to so great misery,
    Binding the living with the dead.
    And now this parting word is said,
We, being twain, may still love on,
Who, being one, had turned to stone ;
    We loose our vows, but link, instead,
Our hearts more surely to love alone.

Olrig Grange, p. 155.

I WOT not what it means ; but now
    The stories of your grey North Sea
Keep running in my head, somehow ;
    And weird and eerie tales they be.
    Was it yourself that told it me?
Or some one else?—I do not know—
How 'mong the isles the tide-waves flow,
    Like maddened steeds that franticly
Are lashed into fury as on they go ;

And how a fisher-lad was once
 Caught in the race, and swept away ;
And how his oars, by evil chance,
 Were reft from him ; and how he lay
 Helpless among the tossing spray :
And how he saw the grim crags loom,
And heard the big waves crash and boom,
 Through mists that darkened on his way,
Darkened and deepened like walls of his tomb ;

And how his heart in him grew cold,
 As still the boat went hurrying on,
Past foaming skerry and headland bold,
 Into the darkness all alone ;
 And weird, witch forms, with eyes of stone,
Looked on, and mocked with laughter dread,
As hungry waves, like fierce wolves, sped,
 And leaped on him ; and hope was none ;
And fain would he pray, but he cursed instead :

And how he lifted up his hand
 To pray or curse, as it might be,
And in that moment grazed the land,
 When something smote his palm, and he
 Grasped a strong rope convulsively—
A fowler's rope that dangled there,
Down on his darkness and despair,
 Barely dipping the swollen sea—
And the half-uttered curse turned into a prayer.

Even so am I on fateful tide
 Borne on, and by the surges tossed,
And helplessly I rock and ride,
 Alone, and in the darkness lost,
 Haunted by many a mocking ghost ;

No help without, no help within,
Forsaken in my way of sin,
   Forsaken by myself the most,
But I reach out in vain through the gloom and
    the din.

   I reach out, but I reach in vain;
    No help for me; I touch the shore;
They only push me back again;
    The tide sweeps on, the waters roar,
    My head is dizzy, my heart is sore;
I reach out, but no help is near,
A cloud is on my soul, and fear,
    And hate and madness evermore
Are hissing their whispers in my ear.

Olrig Grange, p. 159.

EDITORIAL.

BUT now it is not given to any one
To overarch the structure of all knowledge,
And crown it with its dome and golden cross;
Nor is it given to any one to work,
As God does, leisurely, because He draws
Upon the unmeasured ages, wherefore He
Alone may say "'Tis finished, and very good."
We only do a part, and partly well,
And others come and mend it. Thorold tried
Too much for our brief life—a cosmic work,
And toiled to do it in his week of days
That had nor fresh-breathed morn, nor restful eve
For him. So he broke down, a wreck, at last,

Achieving but a fragment of his thought,
A porch, a pillar, and an outline dim.
Some deemed he was a failure ; others saw
The germ of grand discovery in his thought,
And worked it to their profit. Ah ! well, well :
There are who give us all they have, complete,
Nothing omitted, nothing lying behind,
All formulated, tidy, docketed,
Tied neatly up in ribbons, laid in drawers,
And handy for our use—an entire soul,
With all its thoughts booked up to the last hour
In double entry ; these don't interest me ;
I know them, and am done with them ; they have
No infinite possibilities, no shadows
Of the great God upon them, and their light
Is but a row of foot-lights and reflectors
Shining upon the stage, and on themselves.
But others, more aspiring than achieving,
Achieve all in suggestion. They lie down
With Nature, as Ruth lay at the feet of Boaz,
Who longed for his upwaking, and yet feared
What the day-break might bring ; so they with
        dread
And yearning wait, till God shall speak to them
The thing they cannot utter, save in fragments,
In broken strains of angel melody,
Or visions momentary behind the veil ;
Yet more suggestive of Divinity,
More helpful by their infinite reaching forth,
Than all completed thinking. Thorold thus
Pushed at the gates of God, and through the
        chink
Caught, wondering, some gleams of inmost Light
Transcendent, and some cords of harmony

Entrancing; unexpected mysteries
Of unison and beauty, heretofore
Or jarring, or divided, blended now
In reconciling vision of higher truth.

Olrig Grange, p. 171.

LOQUITUR CLAUD MAXWELL.

'Tis the sin of art's fine passion that it only seeks
to know,
Not to perfect, any creature that his lot he may
fulfil;
It has charity to bear with any rankest weeds
that grow
Unto any picturesqueness, and to leave them
growing still.

Priest and prophet try to save, and so their work
is blessed; but mine
Strove only just to see, and reproduce the
picture true,
Making sacrifice of duty for the trimming of a
line,
Heeding not of higher wisdom in the itch for
something new.

O my heart and its misgivings! I am never
wholly sure.
Was the art of Greece so perfect that its life
was also high?
Is the heavenly vision only seen what time the
heart is pure?
Is the poem but the poet as he dares to live
and die?

Could I be a mere onlooker, and yet see what
　　should be seen?
　Standing calmly on the outside, could I paint
　　this life aright?
Nay, that could never come to any perfect fruit,
　　I ween,
　Could yield but sickly blossom nipt by any
　　frosty night.

Better wield a pick or spade, or drive a furrow
　　in the soil,
　Bear a hod, or hurl a barrow among fustian-
　　wearing men,
Win humblest daily bread by daily sweat of
　　honest toil,
　Than live to find in life but stuff for scrawling
　　with a pen !

Hilda, p. 169.

HILDA'S DEATH.

A MIGHTY city of tented streets,
　And never a house of brick or stone,
And the pulse of the city throbs and beats
　As if in a fever burning on ;
Nothing but tents in all the plain,
Nothing but bronzed and bearded men,
With clashing sabre and jingling spur,
Plume of feather, or crest of fur.

Here are banners, and there are flags ;
　All of their bravery now is stained ;
As the wind flutters their tattered rags,
　Lo ! where the powder and blood are grained ;

And the heavy air has a fœtid breath :
Is it of blood? or is it of death?
How the wild dogs and the birds are fat,
Gorged, where they lazily perch or squat !

Now, at a tent-door steeds are champing,
    Now they are galloping forth with speed ;
Down the long streets there are companies tramping,
    Grimly silent, on some fell deed ;
Some in the wine-shop are drinking hard,
Some are gaming with dice and card ;
Many a jolly stave trowls from those,
But these are coming to oaths and blows.

Hark ! to the call of the bugle horn,
    Or the quick rattle of mustering drum !
Swift to the summons, at even or morn,
    Bronzed and bearded, the gallants come.
Balls from the rifle-pits *ping* about,
Great guns boom from the big Redoubt,
And the angry hiss of the burning shell
Screams through the fire and smoke of hell.

Far on the outskirts stands a tent,
    And over the tent a great red Cross ;
Balls lie round, but their force was spent
    Long e'er they rolled o'er the silent moss ;
A cross is over the silent gate,
A cross on the arm of them that wait,
Emblem of pity and healing and peace,
Bidding the wrath of war here to cease.

One comes out of it, grave and sad ;
  Just a whisper, and then returns ;
What are the tidings now? good or bad?
  Still she lives, but the fever burns.
Then again silence reigns all about,
And the twilight pales, and a star comes out,
But yet the air seems to pulse and to throb,
Now and again, with a stifled sob.

Sudden, the sob is turned to a wail ;
  What is it? where is it? Hush ! the door
Opens again now, and all hearts fail ;—
  He too is weeping, for all is o'er.
It is not night, and it is not day ;
Calm in the twilight she passed away,
Just as the star, where the cloud was riven,
Pointed her way through the opening heaven.

Near the tent-door was a sickly group,
  And O the tears ran down their cheeks like
    rain ;
One said, "There is not a man in our troop
  But would have died just to save her a pain :
I would have died for her ; so would a score of
  us ;
Broken and maimed, she was worth many more
  of us ;
God help the poor fellows, now she is gone ;
She was like my mother when last I was down."

When it was told at the drinking bar,
  The flagon untasted was dashed on the board ;
Hushed was the chorus of glory and war—
  Others were trusted, but she was adored.

I

No one shuffled the cards again,
Rattled the dice now, or called a main.
"Who's for the trenches? we must have it out;
Now is the time, lads, to try the Redoubt."

Belted with hell-fire, and shrouded with smoke,
    Girdled with rifle-balls as with a wall,
Yet with a yell from the trenches they broke,
    Plunging through rifle-balls, hell-fire, and all.
'Twas not for glory they stormed the Redoubt;
'Twas that the grief of their wild hearts must out.
That was her monument; and they cried
"God and saint Bridget!" as each man died.

Hilda, p. 241.

THE LETTER.

I BEGGED hard for an hour of grace
    From that grim Ferryman who plies
His wherry to the fore-doomed place
    Of all the foolish and all the wise.
But not an hour the churl will give,
    Nor deigns to answer me, though I,
Who always was in haste to live,
    Would rather take my time to die.

Another sun, and I shall know
    The secret Death has kept so well:
What wonders in a day or so
    A letter writ by me could tell!

And yet who knows? I've mostly found
　　That secrets are but sorry stuff;
And those that lie beneath the ground
　　Perchance are commonplace enough.

I've lived my life; it has not been
　　What once I hoped, nor what I feared;
And why should that we have not seen
　　Be other than has yet appeared?
There are no breaks in God's large plan,
　　But simple growth from less to more;
And each to-morrow brings to man
　　But what lay in the day before.

The river has its cataract,
　　And yet the waters down below
Soon gather from the foam, compact,
　　And on like those above it flow:
And so the new life may begin
　　Where this one stopt, with finer powers,
Perhaps, a subtler thread to spin,
　　And years to work instead of hours.

What has my life been that my heart
　　Should be so tranquil at this time,
So free to ply the careless art
　　Of guessing, and of tagging rhyme?
Here on this solemn brink of doom
　　I seem not much to fear or care,
But peer into the gathering gloom,
　　And mostly wonder what is there.

And that has been my bane all through,
  That never yet would life appear
So real that my hand must do
  Its work with earnestness and fear:
Still I could dream and speculate,
  And turn it somehow into play,
And nothing woke a perfect hate,
  Or love that had its perfect way.

I tried the highest life—and failed;
  A lower, with a small success;
I loved; I sorrowed; laughed and railed
  At Fortune and her fickleness;
And powers I might have trained to grow
  I frittered, for I was not wise;
And now their fire is burning low,
  Their smoke is bitter in the eyes.

Ah! wasted gifts and trifling gains!
  Ah! life that by the abysses played,
And partly knew the griefs and pains
  That from the depths their moaning made,
And partly felt them too, and yet
  Could be content to dream and write,
And jest and laugh, and to forget,
  And never wrought with all thy might!

You'll find in an odd drawer the sum
  Of that life, rich in nought but friends—
A grasshopper's dry-throated hum,
  A hank of broken odds and ends;
Do with it as you will; I give
  My all to you; perchance it may
Beacon another soul to live,
  More wisely through its changeful day.

You'll pay my debts—they are not large ;
   You'll bury me where the poor folk sleep ;
And for the rest, my only charge
   Is that the dear old books you'll keep.
If ghosts come back, mine will be met
   Upon the steps among the shelves,
Searching for mildew, moth, or wet
   In the small quartos or the twelves.

And now farewell, my lad ; fear God,
   And keep your faith whole, if you can,
And where the devil has smoothed your road,
   Keep to the right like an honest man ;
See that your heart is pure and just,
   See that your way is clean and true ;
By and by we shall all be dust,
   Yet by and by I shall meet with you.

The world is losing faith in God,
   And thereby losing faith in man,
For now the earthworm and the sod
   Wind up, they say, our little span ;
But they that hold by the Divine,
   Clasp too the Human in their faith,
And with immortal hopes entwine
   The silence and the gloom of death.

                                     Raban, p. 10.

SERMONS AND MORALITIES.

2 Kings ii. 2-11.

IT was the great Elijah in the chariot of heaven,
With the horses of Jehovah, by a mighty angel
driven,
And the chariot wheels were rushing 'mid a mist
of fiery spray,
Through glory of the night to higher glory of the
day.

It was the great Elijah—but meek and still was he,
For he trembled at the glory which his flesh was
soon to see,
Going, girdled in his sackcloth, as the prophets
were arrayed,
To the splendour of the Presence where the angels
are dismayed.

Unwonted was the honour which his Master would
accord
To His true and faithful witness, bravest servant
of the Lord;
But better had he borne, I trow, the sad old
human way
Of entering by the gates of Death into eternal day.

Ay, better had he borne to turn his face unto
    the wall,
With his kindred in their kindness gathered round
    him, one and all,
And to lie down with his fathers in the dust for
    some brief space ;
For the death, he once had dreaded, now appeared
    a tender grace.

It was the great Elijah ; and the form that would
    dilate
In the presence of King Ahab, and his Councillors
    of State,
Now bowed its head in lowliness, as if it dared
    not cope
With the terror and the glory, and the wonder and
    the hope.

Away from earth they travelled ; yet he somehow
    seemed to know
The road, as if his weary steps had trod it long
    ago :
And was not that the wilderness to which he once
    had fled?
And that the lonely juniper where he had wished
    him dead?

And was not that the cave where he had sat in
    sullen mood,
Until he heard the "still small voice" that touched
    his heart with good?
And was not that the road by which from Carmel
    he had run
Before the chariot of the king about the set of
    sun?

Yea, God was backward leading him to heaven
    along the path
Which he had erewhile travelled o'er in fear or
    grief or wrath,
That by its mingled memories his heart He might
    prepare
For the grandeur and the glory and the crown he
    was to wear.

Now, as they drove, careering, with the fire-flakes
    round the wheels,
And the sparks that rushed like shooting stars
    from the horses' flashing heels,
Lo! he was aware of a throng of men lay strewn
    along the road;
And straight at them the angel drave the chariot
    of God.

" Stay, stay!" then cried Elijah, "rein up the fiery
    steeds;
They will mangle those poor people lying there
    like bruised reeds;
See, they stir not; they are sleeping; or their
    thoughts are far away,
And they do not hear the wheels of God to whom
    perchance they pray.

" Full oft have I been praying so, and chiding
    His delay,
And lo! the work was done, or ere my lips had
    ceased to pray;
For our ears are dull of hearing; stay, and put
    them not to proof
Beneath the grinding of the wheel, and trampling
    of the hoof."

" Nay, it boots not," said the angel, "they are but
the ghosts of those
Three hundred priests of Baalim who fell beneath
thy blows
That glorious day on Carmel ; let them perish, as
they cry
To the gods that cannot help them when they
live, or when they die.

" Drive on, ye horses of the Lord, across the wel-
tering throng,
It is the great Elijah ye are bearing now along,
Let them see him once again in the triumph of his
faith,
And hear the bitter mockery, and taste the bitter
death."

It was the great Elijah, the prophet stern and
grand,
Faithful only to Jehovah he in all the faithless
land,
Zealous even unto slaughter for the God of Israel
'Gainst Ahab and the minions of the Tyrian
Jezebel.

But he answered, " Stay thy running now, and let
me here descend,
For the Lord has brought me hither surely for
this very end :
Ah ! this thing I had forgotten—day of glory and
of dole—
And I wist not what did ail me, but its weight
was on my soul."

Then he stept down from the chariot, looking O so
    meek and mild,
For the burden of the glory made him humble as
    a child;
And he lifted up the prostrate head of one and
    then another,
For the burden of the greatness made him tender
    as a mother.

"Ye priests of ancient Sidon, and of purple Tyre,"
    he cried,
"I have heard a still small voice that hushed the
    storms of wrath and pride,
And God who was not in the fire, and was not
    in the wind,
Was in the still small voice that spake to the
    unquiet mind.

"O worshippers of Ashtaroth, and priests of
    Baalim,
I thought to please Jehovah, and I only grievëd
    Him;
I flouted you, and mocked you, and I deemed
    that I did well
When I smote you in the name of Him, the God
    of Israel.

"But He hath no pleasure in the death of any
    man that dies,
He delighteth not in blood or smoke of such a
    sacrifice;
Yea, not a worm is crushed here, but the writh-
    ings of its pain
Touch a chord of His great pity who made noth-
    ing live in vain.

"He had patience with thee, Sidon, and patience
    I had none ;
For the art of Tyre, perchance, He let the sin of
    Tyre alone,
Something He saw to stay His wrath ; but I
    would nothing see ;
Ye were the priests of Jezebel, and hateful unto
    me.

"I did not think how hard it is to find the way
    of truth;
I did not think how hard it is to shake the faith
    of youth ;
Yet, if I was walking in the light, the credit was
    not mine,
But God's who in His grace to me had made the
    light to shine.

"If ye were walking in the dark, and I was in
    the light,
I should have brought its help to you, and plied
    you with its might;
But I made my heart a flaming fire, my tongue
    a bitter rod,
And I did not hear the still small voice which is
    the voice of God.

"I said ye might have right to live in Tyre
    beside the sea,
But not in high Samaria, or fertile Galilee ;
And I smote you there on Carmel, as I thought,
    by His commands,
But I smote my own heart also when your blood
    was on my hands.

"For the strength departed from me as the pity
in me died,
And in an unloved loneliness I nursed unhallowed
pride ;
And I wist there was none faithful on the earth,
but only I,
And sat beneath the juniper, and prayed that I
might die.

"For Jezebel and Ahab did as they had done
before,
And the idols were exalted, and idolaters were
more,
And the land was nothing better for the blood
that had been shed,
And I sat beneath the juniper, and wished that
I were dead.

"Then it was I heard the still small voice, and
bowed me to the ground,
Humbled by the gracious burden of the mercy I
had found,
But I may not enter into rest, or with the Lord
abide,
Till ye humble with your pardon him that smote
you in his pride."

Then, one by one, he bore them gently from the
angel's way,
And, one by one, he laid them down, and kissed
them where they lay ;
And he never was so human as in his meekness
then,
And he never was so godlike for he was like
other men.

And he said in yearning pity, "O that I might
    die for you,
Hapless souls that are in darkness, and who know
    not what they do!"
And the tearful eye was swimming, and he heaved
    a weary sigh;—
He was very near to glory with that great tear in
    his eye.

And the angel in his chariot sat, and watched
    him toiling long,
And the angel's face shone radiant, and he broke
    into a song;
For the choicest songs of angels are the anthems
    that begin
With the sorrow of a contrite heart a-breaking
    for its sin.

And ever as the prophet wept, the angel sang
    more loud,
And his face was shining more, the more the
    prophet's head was bowed;
Until the task was ended, and the flesh was
    crucified,
When lo! they were at the gate of heaven, and
    the door was opened wide.

Lo! they were at the gate of heaven, and there
    a mighty throng,
Ten thousand times ten thousand, raised their
    shout and sang their song,
But the Lord remembered he was flesh, and down-
    cast for his sin,
And Enoch who had walked with God came forth
    to lead him in.

Raban, p. 97.

THE STANDING STONES.

"God at sundry times and in divers manners spake in time
past unto the fathers."—Heb. i. 1.

A ROLLING upland, open and bare,
  A blasted heath where the night wind moans,
Eerie and weird, to the curlews there,
And the greedy kite and the kestrel scare
Singing birds from the lightsome air.

High on the heath are the Standing Stones,
  Great, gaunt stones in a mystic ring,
Girdling a barrow where heroes' bones
Crumble to dust of death that owns
Them and their wars and faiths and thrones.

Not far off is an oozy spring
  Feeding a black and dismal pool;
There slow efts crawl, horse-leeches cling,
And the dragon-fly whirrs on restless wing,
And near by the adder is coiled in the ling;

And once an oak made a shadow cool,
  Woven of its green boughs overhead,
And blithe birds sang in the leafage full;
Now but a raven, bird of dule,
Croaks on its stump from May to Yule.

But silently watching the silent dead
  Stands the grey circle of sentinels,
Scarred and lichened, as ages sped
With snows, and dripping rains overhead,
And suns, and the wasteful life they bred.

Now, evermore where the dead man dwells
  The living have gone to seek for God,
And the Altar-fire of the Unseen tells,
Or the swing and the clash of Christian bells
Summon to Lauds and Canticles.

And there, of old, in that bleak abode `
  Of wily lapwing and shrill curlew,
To circle and cairn they carried their load
Of burdened thought, as they wearily trod
On to the brink where they lost the road.

There dipped the Sun in the dripping dew
  His earliest beams ; and there he met
The Bel-fire kindling its answer true—
Earth-light for the light in heaven that grew,
Worship-light to the Light-god due.

So men acknowledged, and paid their debt,
  In the old days, to the powers above,
Giving back that they were fain to get,
And piling the faggots, dry or wet,
Still as the keen stars rose and set.

Was not the instinct true that wove
  Fire-worship thus for the god of fire ?
Give from below what ye get from above,
Light for the heaven-light, Love for its Love,
A holy soul for the Holy Dove.

God tunes for Himself the hallowed lyre
  That shall truly His praises show ;
He gives the song that He will desire,
Ever new from the trembling wire,
Ever new from the heart on fire.

Back to its fountain let it flow
  Whatsoever He sends to you ;
Mercy, if mercy of His ye know,
And if your joy He has made to grow,
Up to Him let its gladness go.

So in all faiths there is something true,
  Even when bowing to stock or stone—
Something that keeps the Unseen in view
Beyond the stars, and beyond the blue,
And notes His gifts with the worship due.

For where the spirit of man has gone
  A-groping after the Spirit divine,
Somewhere or other it touches the Throne,
And sees a light that is seen by none,
But who seek Him that is sitting thereon.

Seek but provision of bread and wine,
  High-ceiled houses, and heaps of gold,
Fools to flatter, and raiment fine,
All the wealth of the sea and mine—
And nothing of God shall e'er be thine.

But who seeks Him, in the dark and cold,
  With heart that elsewhere finds no rest,
Some fringe of the skirts of God shall hold,
Though round his spirit the mists may fold,
With eerie shadows, and fears untold.

                       Raban, p. 75.

THE ABBEY.

"God at sundry times and in divers manners spake in time
past unto the fathers."—Heb. i. 1.

NEAR by the river the Abbey stands,
Among old fruit trees, and on fat green lands,
  With a weir on the river to drive the mill,
And cunning cruives at the salmon-leap ;
And the beeves on the clover are fetlock-deep,
  And the sheep are nibbling the grassy hill.

'Tis now but a ruin spreading wide
Broken gable and cloistered side
  'Mong lichened pear-trees and Spanish nuts,
Here a pillar, and there a shrine,
Or niche where its sculptured lords recline :—
  And long a quarry for walls and huts.

O stately the Lady-Chapel there
Once reared its cross in the upper air
  Near by the river among the trees,
And sweet bells rung, and censers swung,
And matins and vespers and lauds were sung
  With solemn-chaunted litanies.

O'er the high Altar a meek face shone,
A virgin-mother and baby-son,
  Fashioned by art beyond the sea ;
And there, in linen or purple dressed,
A priest gave thanks, or a priest confessed,
  With a psalm of praise, or a bended knee.

K

And some would pore over vellum books,
And some would feather the sharp fish-hooks,
   And some would see to the sheep and kine ;
Some went hunting the red-deer stag,
Some would travel with beggar's bag,
   And some sat long by the old red wine ;

Some would go pleading a cause in Rome,
And still found cause to be far from home,
   And near to St. Peter's costly door :
They were not all bad, and they were not all good
Who wore the Monk's girdle and sandal and
    hood,—
   But some of them padded the Cross they bore.

Yet was the Abbey a fruitful stage
In the slow growth, and the ripening age
   Of the long history of man :
For beaming virgin, and holy child
Made many a fierce heart meek and mild,
   And the mastery there of mind began.

The footsore pilgrim there found rest,
The heartsore too was a welcome guest,
   And who loved books, got helpful store.
It is God who guides the world's affairs,
And ever it rises by winding stairs,
   Screwing its way from the less to more.

He reads the story best, who reads
Ever to find some germing seeds
   Sprouting up to a nobler end,
And God's long patience working still
Through all the good, and through all the ill,
   And always something in us to mend.

From bud to bell the wild bee strays,
Seeking the sweets of the sunny days,
    Probing deep for the honey-cell ;
Yet well for his theft he pays the flower,
For he brings to the blossom a quickening power,
    And a richer life to bud and bell.

Narrow and poor was the old Church-life
As it prayed in its cell, amid storm and strife,
    With scourgings many, and fastings new ;
It knew no letters, it spurned at Art,
It had no pleasures, and lived apart—
    Doomed to die as the world's life grew.

But something of wisdom the Monk would know,
Something of gladness here below,
    Something of beauty and what it can ;
He was not sinless, and yet he brought
A larger heart, and a deeper thought,
    And a fuller life to the sons of man.

And we are a stage too—not the end ;
Others will come yet our work to mend,
    And they too will wonder at our poor ways.
Ah ! Life is more than our sermons, prayers,
Bourses, machineries, multiplied wares—
    Still the heart sighs for the better days.

Still is a feeling of something in me
Which yet I am not, and I ought to be,
    Vaguely reaching for more and more ;
And the gain is loss, when I do not win
Larger life for the soul within,
    And hopes of an ever-opening door.

Raban, p. 84.

THE SELF-EXILED.

THERE came a soul to the gate of Heaven
  Gliding slow—
A soul that was ransomed and forgiven,
  And white as snow :
And the angels all were silent.

A mystic light beamed from the face
  Of the radiant maid :
But there also lay on its tender grace
  A mystic shade :
And the angels all were silent.

As sunlit clouds by a zephyr borne
  Seem not to stir,
So to the golden gates of morn
  They carried her :
And the angels all were silent.

" Now open the gate, and let her in,
  And fling it wide,
For she hath been cleansed from stain of sin,"
  St. Peter cried :
And the angels all were silent.

" Though I am cleansed from stain of sin,"
  She answered low,
" I came not hither to enter in,
  Nor may I go :"
And the angels all were silent.

"I come," she said, "to the pearly door,
  To see the Throne
Where sits the Lamb on the Sapphire Floor,
  With God alone :"
And the angels all were silent.

"I come to hear the new song they sing
  To Him that died,
And note where the healing waters spring
  From His pierced side :"
And the angels all were silent.

"But I may not enter there," she said,
  "For I must go
Across the gulf where the guilty dead
  Lie in their woe :"
And the angels all were silent.

"If I enter heaven I may not pass
  To where they be,
Though the wail of their bitter pain, alas!
  Tormenteth me :"
And the angels all were silent.

"If I enter heaven I may not speak
  My soul's desire
For them that are lying distraught and weak
  In flaming fire :"
And the angels all were silent.

"I had a brother, and also another
  Whom I loved well ;
What if, in anguish, they curse each other
  In depths of hell ?"
And the angels all were silent.

" How could I touch the golden harps,
    When all my praise
Would be so wrought with grief-full warps
    Of their sad days?"
And the angels all were silent.

" How love the loved who are sorrowing,
    And yet be glad?
How sing the songs ye are fain to sing,
    While I am sad?"
And the angels all were silent.

"O clear as glass is the golden street
    Of the city fair,
And the tree of life it maketh sweet
    The lightsome air :"
And the angels all were silent.

"And the white-robed saints with their crowns
    and palms
    Are good to see,
And O so grand are the sounding psalms!
    But not for me :"
And the angels all were silent.

"I come where there is no night," she said,
    "To go away,
And help, if I yet may help, the dead
    That have no day."
And the angels all were silent.

St. Peter he turned the keys about,
    And answered grim ;
" Can you love the Lord, and abide without.
    Afar from Him?"
And the angels all were silent.

"Can you love the Lord who died for you,
    And leave the place
Where His glory is all disclosed to view,
    And tender grace?"
And the angels all were silent.

"They go not out who come in here;
    It were not meet:
Nothing they lack, for He is here,
    And bliss complete."
And the angels all were silent.

"Should I be nearer Christ," she said,
    "By pitying less
The sinful living, or woeful dead
    In their helplessness?"
And the angels all were silent.

"Should I be liker Christ were I
    To love no more
The loved, who in their anguish lie
    Outside the door?"
And the angels all were silent.

"Did He not hang on the cursed tree,
    And bear its shame,
And clasp to His heart, for love of me,
    My guilt and blame?"
And the angels all were silent.

"Should I be liker, nearer Him,
    Forgetting this,
Singing all day with the Seraphim,
    In selfish bliss?"
And the angels all were silent.

The Lord Himself stood by the gate,
 And heard her speak
Those tender words compassionate,
 Gentle and meek :
And the angels all were silent.

Now, pity is the touch of God
 In human hearts,
And from that way He ever trod
 He ne'er departs :
And the angels all were silent.

And He said, " Now will I go with you,
 Dear child of love,
I am weary of all this glory, too,
 In heaven above :"
And the angels all were silent.

"We will go seek and save the lost,
 If they will hear,
They who are worst but need me most,
 And all are dear :"
And the angels were not silent.

     Hilda, p. 102.

A CHURCH OF THE AGES.

It is a Church of the Ages, all
 Arched and pillared and grandly towered,
With many a niche on the buttressed wall,
 And delicate tracery, scrolled and flowered :
Gargoyles gape, and arches fly
From base to base of the pinnacles high,
And the great cross points to the solemn sky.

A stately Church, and a Church all through,
  Everywhere shaped by a thought divine,
With symbols of Him who is Just and True,
  And emblems of Him who is Bread and Wine,
It is dowered with wealth of land and gold,
And memories high of the days of old,
And of sheep that were lost gathered into its fold.

Lord bishops sleep their slumber deep
  Under mitre and crosier carved in stone;
There are brasses quaint for the warrior saint
  Who had battled at Acre and Ascalon;
In the low-groined crypts lie kings and earls,
Resting now from their plots and quarrels,
But they mix not their dust with the rustic carles.

It is not day, and it is not dark,
  And the altar-lights are burning dim;
One sings, but it is not priest nor clerk,
  And he chaunts no psalm, and he sings no
    hymn.
Who are these that are trooping in,
With grimy visage, and bearded chin,
Rude and unmannered, with noisy din?

Some one is wailing—a poor soul ailing
  Down in the dim aisles far away;
Who is that droning? is he intoning
  The great Athanasian curse to-day?
Silence that chatter and laughter there,
And do not stand bonneted up to stare—
Hush! that is surely the voice of prayer.

First Voice.

They have made Thy Temple a place abhorred,
  They have mocked Thy Christ, for His own
      betrayed Him;
And now they have taken away my Lord,
  Ah woe! and I know not where they have laid
      Him.

Second Voice.

Now that the gods are certainly dead--
  Brahmâ and Zeus and the Father, and all—
With a desk and a lime-light overhead,
  We might use this up for a lecture-hall.
We could shew them things on the altar there--
  Bringing the light to the proper focus—
Wonderful transformations rare,
  Would beat the priests with their hocus-pocus:
With two or three chemicals we could make
  Nature her miracle-power surrender,
And a glass, at the angle fit, would wake
  A ghost as well as the witch of Endor.
Everything here would give point to my hits
At the monk's huge faith, and his little wits,
As I drive at Bigots, and shout for Truth,
And laugh at the dreams of the world's raw youth.

Third Voice.

A pest on all the reforming crew,
Savant or Puritan, old or new!
See how the rogues come tramping in,
  Now that they have not to praise or pray—

Faugh ! what a breath of tobacco and gin !
They crowd to church because God is away !
And they've smashed that pitying angel's face,
That touched one's heart with its tender grace,
None of their brute-wits can ever replace.
If there be angels good or bad,
I very much doubt, and I do not much care ;
But yet what a pitying look it had,
Beaming down from the oriel there !
Will no one silence that idiot's chatter
About laws, forsooth, of health and riches ?
I'd rather the old priest's "stabat-mater"—
If we had but the ordeal now for witches,
Wouldn't I souse him into the water !

FOURTH VOICE.

Anathema Maranatha ! Hark !
Be he sinner or be he saint,
There is no place in the saving Ark
For one who keeps but a cobweb faint
Of doubt in his heart, or doubt in his head,
About any one article I have read.
"Credo," that is the key of heaven ;
The more incredible, so much more
Virtue lies in the Credo given
To open the everlasting door.
Thurifer, let the censer wave :
" Hoc est corpus," lift it high ;
Christ is risen from the stone-sealed grave ;
Now let us forth with Him, and die
Into the life that comes thereby.
In high procession the priests will go
Chaunting the *Dies Irae* low,

Dies illa, sad and slow.
So the Church in the days of old,
Robed in linen and purple and gold,
Foiled the Devil, and all his tricks,
And drove out the swine with a crucifix.

FIRST VOICE (*far away*).

They have taken away my Lord,
And I know not where they have laid Him!

So it went wailing down the long aisle,
　　Mixed with the hum of the priest and the
　　　　people;
And a shudder passed through the massive pile,
　　From the low-groined crypt to the cross on the
　　　　steeple:
And the glimmering lights on the altar died,
No more the priest-hymn sobbed and sighed,
But a hollow wind wailed through the transept
　　wide.

Hilda, p. 1.

THE VISION OF GOD.

O THE silences of heaven,
　　How they speak to me of God,
Now the veil in twain is riven
　　That concealed where He abode!
Yet its clouds were once around Him,
　　And I sought Him in despair,
And never there I found Him,
　　Till I brought Him with me there.

Not the optic glass revealed Him,
 No mechanical device
Pierced the darkness that concealed Him
 With a vision more precise :
Only lowliness can merit
 That His secret He should tell ;
Only spirit seeth spirit,
 And the heart that loveth well.

Never till His love hath found thee,
 Shall the cloud and mist depart ;
Vain to seek Him all around thee,
 Till He dwell within thy heart.
Not without thee, but within thee
 Must the oracle be heard,
As He seeketh still to win thee,
 And to guide thee by His word.

When I found Him in my bosom,
 Then I found Him everywhere,
In the bud and in the blossom,
 In the earth and in the air ;
And He spake to me with clearness
 From the silent stars that say,
As ye find Him in His nearness,
 Ye shall find Him far away.

Heretic, p. 52.

THE BURDEN OF GOD.

I BORE a load of doubt and care,
 And could not reason it away ;
It might have no right to be there,
 Yet clung to me by night and day.

And I was fain to be alone,
  A stranger in a far off land,
Where friend and helper I had none,
  Nor any that could understand.
O for a glad entrancing faith !
  O for an all-controlling thought
To fill my soul, as with a breath
  That from the Eternal life is brought !
Let me but be alone with God
  A little while on some high place,
Where rarely foot of man hath trod,
  That I may see Him face to face.
So did they long of old, who built
  High altars on the hill-tops bare,
To leave their load of sin and guilt,
  And find the peace they hoped for there.

Then I went toiling up the glen,
  Like one that wanders in a dream,
Past broad-eaved homes of toiling men,
  Along the swiftly rushing stream,
Past the white kirk with ruddy spire,
  And solitary wayside shrine,
Where peasant mothers did admire
  The mother of the Babe divine,
Past orchards where the tawny steer,
  Black-muzzled, stood and whisked his tail,
While men sat in the tavern near,
  With flask of wine or mug of ale.
I heard the sharp *whish* of the scythe, . ,
  And dragging of the patient rake,
I heard the children singing blithe,
  And felt as if my heart would break.

They sang the song of Bethlehem,
  And glad their voices were and clear;
And O that I could sing like them,
  And only knew that God would hear!

Still on, I bore my burden on,
  Finding no help in kirk or shrine,
Or crucifix of carven stone,
  Or picture of the Babe divine:
Alone, I must be all alone,
  Beyond the mighty wooded slopes;
I would have company with none,
  But those vast, silent mountain tops
Which held me with their snowy spell,
  And bade me come to where they stood,
And in their white robes worshipped well
  The Everlasting Pure and Good.

I took the steep rock-path that winds
  Through the pine wood above the stream,—
High up the grey-green glacier grinds,
  Far down its grey-green waters gleam,
A torrent from a neighbouring cliff
  Leaped down, and disappeared half way,
To fall in tremulous mist, as if
  Nature to me was fain to say—
See how the rush of lofty thought,
  The higher that its way appears,
The deeper that its rest is sought,
  Still vanishes in mist and tears.

Still up the rugged path I went,
  With panting breath and trembling knees,
And weary limb, and back low bent,
  Till, past the belt of great pine trees

I came upon a sunny glade
 Open and green, with brooks and wells,
And crocus fields where cattle wade,
 With noise of many jangling bells,
And flat-roofed chalets, piled with stone,
 For winds are boisterous there and wild,
But kirk or steeple there was none,
 Only the Virgin and her Child,
Kept in some homely box for shrine,
 And sheltered in a quiet nook,
Where humble worship might incline
 With bended knee and lowly look.
But all these fond traditions stood—
 How sweet soe'er their tender grace—
Between me and the Pure and Good,
 And I must see Him face to face.

A little speech, a little rest,
 A cup of goat's milk at the door;
Bid me not stay and be your guest,
 There are a good eight hours and more,
Before the sun dips in the west,
 And I must on at any price,
To see his evening glories rest
 Upon the pale green glacier ice,
And on the web of pallid snow,
 That wraps the hills in raiment white,
And on the changing clouds below,
 That catch the fringes of his light.
I did not tell my inmost thought:
 Those neat-herds could not well divine
How I, in search of God, was brought
 Away from kirk and cross and shrine.

Still up and up; the Alpen-stock
    Oft buried in the turf before,
Now smote upon the living rock,
    And from its heart the fire-spark tore ;
And as I trod the gradual slope
    'Neath some snow-crested precipice,
And glanced round with a passing hope
    Of chamois fleet or Edelweiss,
Lo ! then my step grew lightsomer,
    And cheerily I sped along,
And in the brisk and tingling air
    I could have broken into song.
And this I took for omen true,
    That I was on the way of peace,
That doubts were where the pine-woods grew
    And with the haunts of man would cease.

And so at length I trod the snow
    On the hill-top that afternoon,
And saw it in the evening glow,
    And in the sheen o' th' pallid moon,
And saw the wondrous morning dawn
    All rosy on the white-robed peaks
That, ranged·like priest-forms in their lawn,
    Served through eternal holy weeks
About the altar of the Lord,
    Awful in their blanch beauty there,
Silent as if with one accord
    Wrapt in the hush of speechless prayer.
There was no sound of man or beast,
    Nor hum of bee, nor song of bird,
And more the silence seemed increased
    What time the avalanche was heard.

L

Once they had held me with a spell,
  And drawn me with a mystic force,
Those hills, as deeming God must dwell
  There where the waters had their source,
Which made the vales and meadows glad;
  There where in majesty sublime
The changeless snow-clad summits had
  No reckoning of the passing time.
There 'mid the everlasting snow
  Should I not see the eternal right,
And look down on the mists below,
  And gaze up to the fount of light,
And find my burden fall away,
  And feel at last the perfect calm,
That broods in the unchanging day,
  And vision of the great I Am?

But as I stood upon the height,
  I did not find what I had sought,
I did not find the perfect light,
  That answered to my wistful thought;
It did not ease me of my load,
  That I had left the world behind;
I was not any nearer God
  By being far from human kind.
And up amid the bands of ice
  And silent fields of clinging snow,
I could have purchased with a price
  The Virgin and the Babe below.
For not in nature's awfulness,
  And majesty and purity,
And not in her dread silences
  Shall God reveal His depths to thee;

But in a heart that throbs to thine,
 And tongue that speaks a human speech :
The human is the one divine,
 That yearning human souls can reach.
There is no scene of earth fulfils
 The high hope of the soaring mind,
And in the quiet of the hills
 The peace of God I did not find ;
And sweet it was with weary limbs,
 Ere long to sit i' the kirk, and hear
The children singing in their hymns,
 That Christ was come, and God was near.

Heretic, p. 55.

CONTENT.

HOWE'ER it be with some, the broad highway
 Is better than the priestly path for me ;
For when it was my task, from day to day,
To do official pieties, and pray,
 I think I might have grown a Pharisee,
Pumping my heart, when it was dry as dust,
For words of faith and hope—because I must.

Then are we at our highest, when we touch
 The Infinite and Good in worship due,
Bowing in lowly reverence to such
As we deem holiest, and trusting much
 Because the holiest is most pitying too :
Nothing so nobly human as the quest
That seeks true man in God, and there finds rest.

But he who all day handles sacred tasks,
  While his thoughts travail with the world,
    and he
Nor hopes to get from God the thing he asks,
Nor yet to hide from God the heart he masks
  To others—how it wounds his soul to be
Praying-machine, until the day's chief sin
Is the chief duty he, has done therein !

I did not turn a Pharisee ; I fought
  Against the perils that my life beset,
And when I felt no worship, worshipped not,
And when my heart was merry, mirth I sought,
  Entangling jests like gay moths in a net,
And laughed, and made laugh, though I saw, the
    while,
They fancied not a priest so given to smile.

Be the road stormy, be it calm and mild,
  Yet snares are spread there, pitfalls too are dug:
The pious mother, longing that her child
May keep his white robe clean and undefiled,
  Dreams of a peaceful parsonage and snug,
Where the world comes not, neither any snare ;
Yet world and flesh and devil, too, are there.

Just past their teens, we task young souls to do
  What needs a large experience deeply-tried ;
And oft I marvel they remain so true,
Freshening the old, and bringing forth the new,
  And with the growing life still growing wide ;
For the cloud-incense of the altar hides
The true form of the God who there abides.

But now I do my work with hand and head,
  And do my worship with a separate heart ;
With a good conscience earning daily bread,
And by the Heavenly Father duly fed,
  I keep the worship and the work apart ;
And yet the work has worship in it too,
But willing service, not a task I do.

My heart is more at one, my soul more calm,
  My Sunday more a welcome joy to me,
Whose rest is sweetened by the folded palm,
The bended knee, and the uplifted psalm,
  While once it was a fretful troubled sea
Vexed by the thought of human praise or blame,
And only partly lit by the Great Name.

Raban, p. 118.

EARTH WAS WAITING.

" When the fulness of the time was come, God sent
forth His Son, made of a woman."—Gal. iv. 4.

EARTH was waiting, spent and restless,
  With a mingled hope and fear ;
And the faithful few were sighing,
  "Surely, Lord, the day is near ;
The desire of all the nations,
  It is time He should appear."

Still the gods were in their temples
  But the ancient faith had fled ;

And the priests stood by their altars
  Only for a piece of bread;
And the Oracles were silent,
  And the Prophets all were dead.

In the sacred courts of Zion,
  Where the Lord had His abode,
There the money-changers trafficked,
  And the sheep and oxen trod;
And the world, because of wisdom,
  Knew not either Lord or God.

Then the spirit of the Highest
  On a virgin meek came down,
And He burdened her with blessing,
  And He pained her with renown;
For she bare the Lord's Anointed
  For His cross and for His crown.

Earth for Him had groaned and travailed,
  Since the ages first began;
For in Him was hid the secret
  That through all the ages ran—
Son of Mary, Son of David,
  Son of God, and Son of Man.

Hymns, p. 111.

THINK ON ME, LORD.

"Think upon me, my God, for good."—Nehem. v. 19.

THINK on me, Lord; for I am all alone,
  My friends and brethren turn their eyes away;
Who love me, fear to let their love be known;
  Who hate me, boast that none shall say them
      nay;
  Think on me, Lord, and open up my way.

They watch my steps—my steps do always err;
  They catch my words—no word of mine is true;
Mine every look hath something sinister;
  And what lacks meaning they give meaning to;
  Think on me Lord; I wot not what to do.

Think on me, Lord; I lift mine eyes above,
  And reach out in the darkness for Thy light,
And reach out in my loneliness for love,
  And in my weakness reach to Thee for might;
  Think on me, Lord, alone in the dark night.

I think on Thee, whom all forsook and fled,
  And on the loneliness of Love divine,
And of the thorns they plaited for Thy head;
  And then I think how light are griefs of mine,
  Yea, glorious being a fellowship with Thine.

Think on me, Lord; for in the name of Him
  Whose name is Love, they compass me with
      hate;
Think on me, Lord; and in my darkness trim
  The lamp within, that I may calmly wait,
  Loving the more the more disconsolate.

Hymns, p. 46.

ONE THING I OF THE LORD DESIRE.

"Blessed are the pure in heart: for they shall see God."
Matt. v. 8.

ONE thing I of the Lord desire—
    For all my way hath miry been—
Be it by water or by fire,
    O make me clean.

Erewhile I strove for perfect truth,
    And thought it was a worthy strife;
But now I leave that aim of youth
    For perfect life.

If clearer vision Thou impart,
    Grateful and glad my soul shall be;
But yet to have a purer heart
    Is more to me.

Yea, only as the heart is clean
    May larger vision yet be mine,
For mirrored in its depths are seen
    The things divine.

I watch to shun the miry way,
    And stanch the spring of guilty thought;
But, watch and wrestle as I may,
    Pure I am not.

So wash Thou me without, within;
    Or purge with fire, if that must be;
No matter how, if only sin
    Die out in me.

Thoughts and Fancies, p. 3.

BE STILL.

"Commune with your own heart upon your bed, and
be still."—Ps. iv. 4.

BE still, and know He doeth all things well,
  Working the purpose of His holy will,
And if His high designs He do not tell
  Till He accomplish them—do thou be still.

Why should'st thou strive and fret and fear and
    doubt,
  As if His way, being dark, must bode thee ill?
If thine own way be clearly pointed out,
  Leave Him to clear up His, and be thou still.

Was ever yet thy trust in Him misplaced?
  And hoping in Him, did He not fulfil
The word on which He causëd thee to rest,
  Though not as thou had'st thought, perchance?
  Be still.

What if the road be rough which might be
    smooth?
  Is not the rough road best for thee, until
Thou learn by patient walking in the truth
  To trust and hope in God, and to be still?

A little faith is more than clearest views ;
  Would'st thou have ocean like a babbling rill?
God without mystery were not good news ;
  Wrestle not with the darkness, but be still.

Be still, and know that he is God indeed
  Who reigns in glory on His holy hill,
Yet once upon the Cross did hang and bleed,
  And heard the people raging—and was still.

Thoughts and Fancies, p. 21.

LORD, I WOULD CHOOSE.

"Mary hath chosen that good part."—Luke x. 42.

LORD, I would choose the better part
  Which none may take away from me;
Let me not fret with anxious heart,
  But sit at peace, and hold with Thee
Communion sweet here at Thy feet.

There be that love Thee well and true,
  And yet they vex their souls with care;
For still much service they will do,
  And many needless vessels bear,
And they with such are cumbered much.

They love Thee, Lord, and Thy good word,
  Yet of Thy joy they stint their heart,
And grudge the peace Thou dost accord
  To them that choose the better part;
And, idly faint, they make complaint.

The one thing needful let me do,
  Nor let my service cumber me;
Who serve the Lord must hold in view
  They need Him more than needeth He;
Who serve Him best in Him too rest.

So would I rest, Lord, at Thy feet,
  And learn of Thee, and look above;
Doing the service that is meet,
  But free to worship and to love,
And find increase of grace and peace.

Hymns, p. 153.

HE LED ME OUT AND IN.

"He shall go in and out, and find pasture."—John x. 9.

HE led me out and in,
And pasture still I found,
    For where He led me
    There He fed me,
Although it might seem barren ground.

He led me out and in,
Yet in the frost and cold,
    With Him beside me
    To cheer and guide me,
My peace was great as in the Fold.

He led me out and in,
From many a hallowed spot
    To buying, selling,
    Planting, felling,
And yet my spirit fainted not.

He led me out and in,
And if to-day was glad,
    While to-morrow
    Brought its sorrow,
Yet they both a blessing had.

So lead me out and in :
Thy guidance, Lord, is best ;
If Thou chasten
'Tis to hasten
My footsteps to the promised rest.

And in the Fold or out,
It shall be well with me
Or in sadness,
Or in gladness,
If only I am still with Thee.

Thoughts and Fancies, p. 16.

LORD, WE ARE PILGRIMS.

"They confessed that they were strangers and pilgrims
on the earth."—Heb. xi. 13.

LORD, we are pilgrims here,
    Resting a night ;
Waiting our call to hear
    At morning light ;
Humble our fare may be,
Thankful no less are we,
Parting more easily
    From small delight.

Lord, we are pilgrims poor ;
    But Thou art right,
He goeth nimblest sure
    Who goeth light ;

Riches we would not heap,
Burdens they were to keep,
Cares only should we reap
  By day and night.

Lord, we are pilgrims true,
  Nor would go back ;
E'er since Thy love we knew
  Nothing we lack ;
Dark is the earth with sin,
And we would glory win,
Let not our pace begin
  Now to be slack.

Lord, we are pilgrims all,
  Hastening to Thee ;
Forward, whate'er befal,
  Our path must be ;
Our home in Heaven is,
Glory and blessedness,
Rest and eternal peace
  There we shall see.

Lord, do Thou bring us all
  Back when we stray ;
And let us never fall
  Out by the way ;
Still let us sing Thy praise,
Still serve the God of grace,
Still do with cheerfulness
  What good we may.

Hymns, p. 91.

Poems by the Same Author.

OLRIG GRANGE. Fourth Edition. 5s.

HILDA. Fourth Edition. 5s.

KILDROSTAN. 5s.

THOUGHTS AND FANCIES FOR SUNDAY EVENINGS. Second Edition. 2s. 6d.

A HERETIC AND OTHER POEMS. 7s. 6d.

www.ingramcontent.com/pod-product-compliance
Lightning Source LLC
Chambersburg PA
CBHW032011060726
47497CB00017B/2967